Gold, Silver, and Guns

Gold, Silver, and Guns

A Novel

George E. Smith

iUniverse, Inc.
New York Lincoln Shanghai

Gold, Silver, and Guns

Copyright © 2007 by George E. Smith

All rights reserved. No part of this book may be used or reproduced by any means, graphic, electronic, or mechanical, including photocopying, recording, taping or by any information storage retrieval system without the written permission of the publisher except in the case of brief quotations embodied in critical articles and reviews.

iUniverse books may be ordered through booksellers or by contacting:

iUniverse
2021 Pine Lake Road, Suite 100
Lincoln, NE 68512
www.iuniverse.com
1-800-Authors (1-800-288-4677)

Because of the dynamic nature of the Internet, any Web addresses or links contained in this book may have changed since publication and may no longer be valid.

Certain characters in this work are historical figures, and certain events portrayed did take place. However, this is a work of fiction. All of the other characters, names, and events as well as all places, incidents, organizations, and dialogue in this novel are either the products of the author's imagination or are used fictitiously.

ISBN: 978-0-595-46084-7 (pbk)
ISBN: 978-0-595-70074-5 (cloth)
ISBN: 978-0-595-90384-9 (ebk)

Printed in the United States of America

RIBERA

Arizona in Territorial Days
and the Clash Between
Native Americans, Mexicans,
Ranchers and Prospectors
for Water, Land and Minerals

George Smith

CHRONOLOGY

1821	Mexico gains independence from Spain
1836	Santa Anna defeats Texans at the Alamo
1845	U.S. Mexican War
1848	Treaty of Guadalupe Hidalgo; U.S. acquires Texas, New Mexico, Arizona, Utah, Nevada, and California
1849	California "Gold Rush"
1850	Territory of New Mexico (New Mexico, Arizona) established
1853	Gadsden Purchase
1859	Comstock silver lode discovery in Nevada
1861	Start of Civil War; army posts abandoned in West
1861	Apache, U.S. Army battle at Apache Pass, New Mexico
1863	Arizona becomes separate Territory; gold discovered at LaPaz
1864	Navajo surrender at Canyon de Chelly
1865	Civil War ends
1870	Arizona Territory population estimated at 9,658

PROLOGUE

The story of Ribera (Riverbank) is the early history of people struggling to survive and prosper during the 1860's in southern Arizona. The domination of Spanish and Mexican rule is beginning to wane; Indians are being squeezed on to reservations against their will. Miners are streaming into the territory from the West; homesteaders and ranchers are arriving daily from the East to start new lives. The Americanization of the great Southwest is underway.

Indians were the first inhabitants of the area known as Arizona today. The Papagos, Pimas and Apaches thrived in the Santa Cruz, San Pedro and Gila river valleys, growing corn and melons, raising dogs and turkey for meat and hunting small animals with bows and arrows. The wheel was unknown to them. When the Spaniards moved northward into the Sonoran desert, they brought with them sheep, goats, pigs, cattle, chickens, donkeys and horses. They also attempted to catholicize the natives, while searching for precious metals. In spite of repeated expeditions to locate the "Seven Cities of Cibola," they failed to find gold and silver on any scale resembling Peru and Mexico.

Criss-crossing southern Arizona, the Spanish padres established missions and built the presidio of Tucson. It was the introduction of the horse that gave the Indians new mobility and the ability to wage guerilla warfare as we know it today. The Apaches, in particular, were a constant threat to farmers, ranchers and prospectors.

Spanish explorers, Indians and Mexicans lived in Arizona for over 300 years before Americans arrived. Mexico gained its independence from Spain in 1821, but did little to develop its northernmost border. Texas independence eventually sparked a war between the U.S. and Mexico, which was settled in 1848 (Treaty of

Guadalupe Hidalgo). Mexico ceded Texas, New Mexico, Arizona, Utah, Nevada, parts of Colorado and all of California. In 1853, the U.S. forced the sale of Arizona land south of the Gila River to its present boundary. The loss of this huge expanse of land kept U.S.-Mexican relations at the boiling point until Pancho Villa was subdued in 1912.

During the 1850–1860 period, Arizona was only sparsely populated. Tucson and Yuma were major towns in the south, Phoenix was barely a spot landing along the Salt River. People moved from place to place by horseback, stagecoach or riverboat on the Colorado River. Few crossed the "Camino Diablo," the brutal desert expanse between Yuma and Tucson, where summer temperatures reached 120 degrees and water holes were seasonal and difficult to locate. To the east of Tucson, Apache tribes roamed almost at will, particularly during the Civil War, when Army troops were redeployed East to fight the Confederacy.

In spite of the hostile environment, the temptation of "striking it rich" lured prospectors from California and Nevada to the LaPaz area where placer gold was discovered in early 1862. Gradually, they drifted toward Tucson and beyond, establishing mining districts in Nogales, Patagonia and Harshaw.

The river valleys also attracted homesteaders and ranchers to southeastern Arizona. Adequate year-round water, good pasture land and moderate temperatures allowed newcomers to take advantage of the Homestead Act (1861) and the government's plan to develop the country from the Mississippi River westward to the Pacific Ocean.

The clash between disenfranchised Indians, Mexicans, invading farmers and ranchers and miners was inevitable. Eventually, the U.S. Army forced the containment of the Navajos, Apaches and Yavapais onto reservations, but only after a twenty-year guerilla war that ended with the surrender of Geronimo in 1886. At the same time, ranchers, farmers and miners also fought each other over land, water and mineral rights.

This is the environment in southern Arizona in the 1860's: desolate deserts, rugged mountains, rampaging Apaches, tiny pockets of population fighting for survival against all odds. These territorial days tested early pioneers almost beyond human endurance.

AGUIJADOR

The vapors from a lingering fire diffused as they journeyed to the smokehole of the wickiup. A small pile of mesquite logs was being used to keep the fire alive to provide some heat and light for the two Indians inside. Outdoors, rapidly cooling temperatures in the night air signaled that winter was not very far away. The tribe, led by Gray Wolf, was ill-prepared for the change in season; food supplies and blankets were perilously low. The white boss at the trading post was stealing their rations, but complaints to the army troop went unheeded. The senior chieftains, well aware of the decimation of their followers, were still undecided as to how to deal with General Barnstable and the U.S. Army, who were steadily pressuring the tribe on to marginal hunting and farm land.

Aguijador lay semi-conscious on the bearskin robe as the Chiricahua Apache shaman applied a poultice of creosote oil, calcareous mud and pinon paste to his shoulder wound. He'd earned the bearskin as a young buck, single-handedly stalking and killing the animal with a lance and hunting knife. It confirmed his passage to adulthood and full warrior status, while still in his youth. His shoulder was still very sore. The bullet, fired by a U.S. soldier, had entered his body, ripping through flesh and muscle cleanly, without striking bone. Cauterization of the painful injury with a heated iron rod had shocked the warrior into unconsciousness, while he clenched his teeth on a thick leather strap. But now, as his head began to clear, Aguijador realized that he was one of the few survivors of the deadly ambush.

A week earlier, a small band of warriors had skirted Fort Gore and crossed into Old Mexico in search of stray mustangs. They would also be on the lookout for a lone cow or two, which would be butchered in the field and eaten or dried into pemmican. Every effort would be made to increase the tribal food supply for the upcoming winter.

The ride into Old Mexico had been successful. To add to their good hunt, they had also stolen a dozen or so horses from a corral in the village of Cordizo, Sonora. When barking dogs had aroused the villagers, the Indians rode hard to escape the wrath of the enraged ranchers, who were surprisingly well armed. Aguijador was pleased to learn that, fortunately, they were also poor marksmen. The horse thieves were able to make a clean escape, crossing the border into the Sulphur Springs Valley of Arizona. As they moved into the foothills of the Dragoon Mountains, the Indians, with their herd of mustangs and stolen Mexican horses in tow, ran into a fusillade of U.S. Army rifle fire.

Several days earlier, an Apache turncoat scout had learned of the trip into Mexico and helped plot an attack on the returning braves. The troopers were positioned in a narrow canyon, strewn with huge sandstone boulders on both sides of the trail. As the Indians led the horses into the ambush site, the soldiers, well hidden behind the rocks, opened fire without warning on the raiding party, instantly killing the two lead braves. In the brief, but deadly, firefight that followed, Aguijador and two other Indian horsemen were wounded, as the frightened ponies scattered to escape the battle. In a second volley, Aguijador's horse was killed and he escaped only by jumping on the back of Smart Eyes's animal. As the two Indians raced through the exit of the pass, Lt. Caswell murmured to himself, "That old scout was right; them injuns are cowards when caught in a fight. Well, we got most of 'em, their horses and whatever supplies they were carrying. It's been a good day."

As Aguijador and Smart Eyes reached the safety of the tribal outpost, the chieftain tried to reconstruct the morning's disaster. The loss of three senior warriors, thirty horses and food, added up to a serious loss to the tribe. Most confusing, the Apaches had recently signed a new treaty with the Army that should have prevented such a happening. Still in shock, he asked himself, why had the soldiers attacked his party? Had something happened between the settlers and his tribe while they were in Old Mexico? How did the troopers know their route of return; the ambush site was very close to Indian territory which the Army normally stayed clear of. Had Gray Wolf's hidden camp been discovered? The more he thought about the surprise battle, the more he believed that the white man was up to his old trick of signing a new treaty, then breaking his word under some false excuse. "How many times will we be deceived before we understand that the white man is only out to steal our land, our food supply and water holes? We are fools to trust the white invaders. We are a warrior nation and must fight to get back our land or we will surely perish on some desolate reservation."

Unknown to Aguijador, a week earlier a white settler had wrongfully claimed that a marauding band of Chiricahua Apache Indians had kidnapped his son. When he'd discovered his son's absence, Dell Butler had ridden to Fort Gore to report the incident and, in a rage, demanded that the Army should chase down the savages before they got away. Unknown to the senior Butler, his son had ridden away from the ranch by himself, "sick and tired of ranch life and fed up gettin' ordered around all the time by a good for nothin' old man." While Butler Senior was cussing out the U.S. Army for dereliction of duty, his son had made it to Tucson and the Mexicana Cantina, where he was working hard at getting drunk on cheap tequila, looking forward to the evening's festivities with the senoritas. He had no intention of ever returning to the Butler ranch.

Captain Hiram Coolidge, the fort commander, was away from the base when Dell Butler made his complaint to Lieutenant Caswell. Jeremy Caswell, fresh out of the U.S. Military Academy at West Point, was an eager listener, hoping for an opportunity to spill some Indian blood. Without a detailed verification that Dell Butler was being truthful, the young officer decided to act immediately. Summoning Sergeant Vince Booker, he ordered the NCO to make ready for a march to intercept the "kidnappers." When Sergeant Booker cautioned the young officer, Caswell stared at the veteran, saying: "We were sent here to protect people like Mr. Butler and I'm going to do just that. If we allow the Apache to attack our ranchers and homesteaders, we'll never be able to get this country under control. This man's son has been taken by Apaches and we're going after 'em. I'm not gonna wait for the C.O. to return. We don't know how long he'll be away and we're already losing time. Get me two squads of horsemen, provisioned for a week's ride and let's be on the trail by noontime."

Silently, Sergeant Booker accepted the order and hiked to the bunkhouse, wondering, "Just what trail does the Lieutenant have in mind? What in hell do they teach these people at West Point? It's no wonder that casualties are so high among new officers in the West."

With the help of renegade Apache defectors, Lt. Caswell had learned about Aguijador's provisioning expedition into Old Mexico. Relishing the idea of a major victory, the troopers had set up their ambush just before the Apaches made their way back to Gray Wolf's mountain hideout. The ambush had surprised the weary group of tribesmen. When the battle was over, the dead and wounded Indians counted and the captured food and horses tallied, it was clear that Lt. Caswell had scored a major victory. Unfortunately, it didn't solve the disappearance of Dell Butler's son, but a victory over the Apaches was a victory, to be savored by any new lieutenant assigned to Indian Territory. No doubt the Captain would be pleased with his report of the action. The only person who avoided the celebration was Sergeant Booker. He knew that Gray Wolf and Aguijador would find out who had assisted in the ambush and would demand punishment for breaching their agreement with the Army. Retaliation for this injustice would be unpredictable, but severe.

In the safety of Gray Wolf's stronghold in the rugged Dragoon Mountains, the chieftain continued to ponder what had happened. He was bitter over the loss of his braves, food and horses, but more important, realized that the tribe was being methodically exterminated. "Gray Wolf is a fierce warrior when antagonized. With another broken agreement, why does our leader withdraw to his wickiup to think over what the white man is up to? It's clear to all that winter is coming on and we are not going to have the food that we need. We have been promised provisions and warm blankets, but they never seem to reach us. It's also clear that Army agreements are worthless, to be changed whenever they want to allow more ranchers, settlers and miners to come in and take over tribal lands. Time and time again, we have been pushed away from good crop land and our best hunting grounds. Surely Gray Wolf knows this; why is he not willing to gather our remaining warriors and fight to save our land? If Gray Wolf is going to allow our nation to be destroyed, who will save us?"

Long, long ago in the early sixteenth century, Spaniards had explored the Sonoran Desert, seeking gold and silver, and hoping to convert the native population to Catholicism. They had marched northward from Mexico bringing with them horses, goats, cattle and sheep. Missions were established at Tubac, San Xavier and Tucson while the main body moved north, searching for the "Seven Cities of Gold," that had eluded discovery. Northern Mexico and what is now Arizona and New Mexico was a vast area of desert, mountains and important river valleys. These rivers, the Santa Cruz, San Pedro and Gila, provided the water to support a large number of small animals, fish and moisture for farming. The Apache tribes thrived in this environment, while ignoring the outcroppings of copper, gold and silver.

The main establishment was the presidio at Tucson, which had about 700 inhabitants in the late 1850's. They were mostly Mexicans, who eked out a subsistence living by farming and trading with the Pima and Apache Indians. The treaty of Guadalupe Hidalgo in 1853 changed the boundary between Old Mexico and the Territory of New Mexico (which included Arizona), but did little to change the population and culture in the desert area. Before the Civil War, the

U.S. Army established forts in the area, but most of these were abandoned when the war heated up in the East.

Late in The 1850s, prospectors, failing to strike it rich in California, began drifting southeast to the Colorado River and Arizona. Placer gold was discovered north of Yuma and a small invasion of prospectors swarmed into LaPaz and central Arizona. Gradually, miners moved to the east looking for metals in the Nogales-Tucson area. This shift in population upset the tenuous peace that existed between the Indians, Mexicans and scattered groups of farmers and ranchers. At the same time, settlers from the Midwest were moving into the Territory. These incursions of white people were relentless. Sometimes by persuasion, other times by force, the Indians retreated from the best land that supported crops and wild animals. Federal policy encouraged the migration of people westward and connecting the East with the unpopulated West. The Mescalero and Chiricahua Apaches battled these invasions fiercely for over twenty years before Geronimo surrendered in 1886.

During the Civil War period, the Apache tribes took over southern Arizona, raising havoc with civilians and the few scattered, undermanned Army forts. At Apache Pass, New Mexico Territory, on July 15, 1862, federal troops were attacked by Cochise and 700 Apache warriors and barely escaped a massacre. As the Civil War continued in the East, fewer and fewer soldiers were available to protect a huge geographic area. The Indians were on the warpath throughout the state. Not until the Navajos surrendered in 1864 and Mangas Coloradas was killed, did some degree of military control succeed.

Mexico, still bitter over the loss of Texas, New Mexico, Arizona, Utah, Nevada and California after losing the war with the U.S., smoldered over the forced Gadsden Purchase, seethed over Apache raiding parties invading their northern borders, but could do little to stop the incursions. With the Arizona border over 1300 miles from Mexico City, the states of Sonora and Chihuahua were virtually defenseless against American Indians and Mexican bandits. Many huge land grant concessions conferred by Spanish royalty were invalidated or ignored by U.S. interests. Boundaries were redrawn and land simply confiscated by newly arrived ranchers and settlers. The law was non-existent.

Ribera (bank on the river), a small town between El Paso and Tucson, began as a rest stop for the Overland Stage Line. The route originated in St. Louis, Missouri, went through San Antonio and El Paso, Texas; then on to Tucson and Yuma, Arizona, then westward to San Diego. The region between El Paso and Tucson was desolate, rugged and in constant danger of Indian attack. High mountains and steep uncharted canyons provided the Apaches with plenty of cover to intercept, rob and kill innocent travelers. U.S. Army patrols were sporadic and local peace officers stayed close to home. Ribera prospered due to the Bowie River, which provided water for ranching, farming and large scale placer mining of gold. As people moved into the territory, they learned to enjoy the moderate climate and access to water, staying on to grow with the town. Stories of summer heat reaching 120 degrees in the desert area between Tucson and Yuma also were a strong influence to settle permanently in the new community of Ribera.

As Aguijador began to recover from his shoulder wound, he talked with tribal elders about the coming cold weather, the prospect of starving families and aggressive U.S. Army actions with the tribe. Most of the senior Indians were skeptical of reports that hundreds of Navajos had perished after their surrender at Canyon DeChelly. The chieftain couldn't convince anyone that the Army's main objective was to destroy the Apache nation. After several days of fruitless discussion, he concluded that open warfare with the government forces was the only possible solution to survival. More and more blue coats were being transferred to the West, now that the Civil War had ended. Many of these Union soldiers were battle hardened veterans who, he believed, would be stronger adversaries. "But, how can I convince our leadership that believing the white man's treaties and promises will only hasten our transfer to a reservation or our death?" Uniting the nation to fight for their existence didn't have a ready solution.

When gold was discovered on the Bowie River, prospectors swarmed into the outskirts of Ribera to seek their fortune. One of these individuals was Tom Lawson, a veteran of many such forays in California, Nevada and LaPaz. He was a loner who staked his claim and quickly went to work, sifting sand and gravel in hopes of spotting a nugget of gold. After a week of sampling, Tom had to conclude that his stake was barren, or close to it. He'd been able to extract enough tiny particles to keep himself in food and tools, but recognized that it was time to move on. Besides, the riverbed was getting overcrowded and poaching was becoming prevalent. When the miner adjacent to his claim offered him two gold coins worth fifty dollars, Tom sold out and moved on. After the first good meal he'd had in a week, he took a room for the night to collect his thoughts. Next morning, he decided to move up river and get away from the crowd to continue his prospecting. It was at the confluence of the Bowie River and Growler Creek that Tom Lawson learned the difference between gold and silver.

BEN LAWSON

The letter had been mailed from Tucson, Arizona; New Mexico Territory, over a month ago. The envelope was crinkled and splattered with dirt, but the handwriting was unmistakable. Tom Lawson, my older brother, had left Denver over four years ago to seek his fortune in the goldfields of California. Ever since gold had been discovered at Sutter's Mill, Tom was obsessed with the idea of prospecting as a means of livelihood. He believed and dreamed of "striking it rich" and that it was only a matter of hard work, luck, and perseverance. We hadn't heard a word from Tom in those four years. Dad, a practicing physician, figured he could be in Alaska, digging for opals in Australia, or a casualty of some bar room brawl only God knows where. At one point a few years ago, we had him located in Cedar City, Utah, but attempts to reach him had been futile.

Early on, it was apparent that Tom didn't enjoy school work and had no interest in the field of medicine. Even as a youngster, he would play hooky from school, and, off on his own, would prospect for mineral specimens at old mine dumps or be chipping samples from a rock outcrop. He was big for his age at six feet tall, two hundred pounds, and kept himself in good physical condition. When he reached fourteen, he told the Doc the inevitable: "Dad, I'm not cut out to be a doctor and there's no sense you wasting money on something I'm not interested in. I can read, write, and do my sums, which is all the education I think I'm gonna need. I guess by now you know that I'm not looking for city living for the rest of my life."

Now Doc Lawson, our Dad, could be stubborn at times, but on this occasion, he could see the handwriting on the wall. He told Tom: "You know I hoped you'd be a doctor and join me, working together. There will always be a need for doctors as the West grows and your mother always saw you as a doctor or maybe a lawyer. By the same token, I'm not going to force you into something you don't want to do. Heck, at fourteen, I told my Dad in Ohio I wasn't going to be a farmer like him. That's when I packed up and went to St. Louis. Luckily, I got work in a dentist's office and, eventually, got to hang out my own shingle. Tom, give yourself a chance to see if you really want to be a miner. Don Sells runs the local assay office and I know he could use a hand to prepare samples and run errands for him in the field. Work with him for six months and then let's talk."

Reluctantly, Tom agreed to Dad's proposition and went to work for Don Sells. The exposure to identifying minerals and talking to real prospectors and old sourdoughs only increased his resolve to get into the field on his own. Halfway through the trial period, Dad conceded defeat and agreed to let Tom sign on with a wagon train that was headed for California. Tom was ecstatic, Dad was misty-eyed, and I was feeling low because I couldn't go with him as we said our goodbyes.

A few weeks after Tom's departure, Dad asked me to join him in his study. He told me about his younger years as a dentist, then becoming a doctor and how things were changing. The Civil War had significantly accelerated medical technology and training for new doctors was being upgraded. For the first time, he shared what he went through when Mom was killed in a wagon accident, his grieving and decision to remain single. He'd hired widow Ebbie Bailey to run the household and raise two boys while he immersed himself in building a successful practice. As the evening wore on, Dad also confessed that he was slowing down and looking for someone to help him gradually work fewer hours and eventually succeed him. He struggled with the words, but in a roundabout manner, finally got to the point of our discussion.

"I would very much like to see you be that person, but I don't want you to do it unless you really want to. I don't want to see you enter a profession, just because I want you to. The training will not be easy and the best place to study would take you away from here for at least four years. I know you're up to it if you decide to be a doctor, but is that what you want to do?"

With Tom refusing the opportunity, I'd spent many hours trying to decide about my future. By the time Dad got around to asking, I'd pretty much decided that I wanted to be a doctor, specializing in surgery. Dad was thrilled when I told him that medicine was my choice and that eventually I looked forward to working with him in Denver.

At age seventeen, after completing local schooling, I boarded the stage for St. Louis. Ebbie cried, Dad shook my hand with the remark, "Son, you have all the tools needed to be a good doctor. You're going to get training I never even dreamed of, so make the most of it. Keep in touch and make your mother proud." Ebbie had me well stocked with food for the nine-hundred mile trip eastward to the Mississippi River and the Missouri College of Medicine.

The studies were difficult at first, but by the end of three months, I understood the routine and began to study more efficiently. The professors with wartime experience doctoring with the battlefield wounded were the most interesting instructors. Part of my formal training involved specialization in anatomy and surgical procedures, using cadavers where the odor of formaldehyde could be nauseous at times. These studies enabled me to eventually intern at a hospital in southwest Missouri, where a huge deposit of lead and zinc was being mined. For a six-month period, I worked at the hospital and the company clinic, doing twelve-hour shifts in the emergency ward. Here, I set broken bones, performed several amputations and treated burns suffered by miners working underground. The miners worked five hundred feet below the surface, where wall rock temperatures were over one hundred degrees. Poor lighting, inadequate ventilation, noxious fumes and the movement of heavy equipment presented a constant hazard. It was hard, dangerous and dirty work. Serious injury and death were all too common. There were no underground first-aid stations, so on several occasions I went to the bowels of the mine in a cage, which rapidly transported rescue teams to the level where the accident had happened. One time, smoke and fumes prevented us from reaching the injured in time, and twelve families were left without fathers and a paycheck. During this period, I learned to appreciate the experience of our teachers at the college who had been part of the Union Medical Corps.

When I was finally awarded a medical doctor diploma, I returned to Denver, ready to join Dad in his practice. Dad and Ebbie had aged a bit, but were in good health and welcomed me with open arms. It wasn't long before I was accompanying Dad on his regular rounds. He was expert in diagnosing problems and had a very pleasant way with people he'd known for over twenty years. He taught me a lot about family diseases; I worked mostly with sprains, broken bones and surgeries. We worked hard, long days, but enjoyed our work together immensely. We developed a good balance and I could see Dad begin to relax some. Tom's letter was about to wreck this equilibrium.

In his lengthy note, Tom apologized for not writing, but explained that he was always too far away from a town to post a letter. He then went on to tell Dad that it looked like his time had finally arrived and that he'd "struck it rich." About three months ago, while prospecting for placer gold, he'd discovered hard rock laced with veinlets of silver. At first, he wasn't sure of what he had, because all the locals were focused on looking for gold. However, he did recall that people in Nevada had overlooked the Comstock Lode, until one suspicious miner had the soft bluish rock analyzed. The rest was history. The Comstock silver deposit became one of the richest finds in American mining history.

Still uncertain of what he'd discovered, Tom decided to stake a claim, fearful that poachers would learn of his find. Discovery secrets didn't last long in places like Tent City, where hundreds of prospectors were scouring the countryside looking for a strike that would make them rich. After recording his claim in Copper Flats, Tom sent ore samples to Silver City, New Mexico, for analysis. When he received the assay report, he was shocked to learn that his samples ran seven hundred dollars per ton, a very rich find indeed! Tom let out a hoot of joy, then tried to figure out his next move. Not trusting of potential local investors, whom he didn't know anyway, Tom decided to turn to his family for money that would enable him to develop the property. Maybe he also felt a little guilty over the past four years away from Denver without writing a single word to the family. Until he'd heard from Dad, he would continue to drive the tunnel and stay onsite to protect his claim.

"I've got two Mexican miners who are helping me at the present time. As far as I know, my discovery is still a secret in Ribera, which is twenty miles downstream. I feel pretty secure with a rifle and two Colt navy pistols, and so far we haven't had any visitors. I'm positive I've discovered something big, but it's going to take money to find out just how big. If possible, I'd like to have Ben come down here to help me for a year or so. I will need someone I can trust buying supplies, hiring people and setting up transportation to get the ore to the smelter in Copper Flats, while I do the mining."

As mentioned earlier, Tom didn't spend much time explaining where he'd been in the last four years or his writer's cramp.

Dad's reaction to the letter was loud and explosive. "Here it's been four years since I've heard from this guy and out of the blue, he wants $5,000 to open a mine. What the hell does he think I am; some rich banker, with more money than brains? How in hell am I supposed to believe he's found a mountain of silver in some rat hole in the Arizona desert? Away all this time and suddenly he needs $5,000 and wants to hear from us right away. I don't believe this!"

Now in fairness to Dad, he'd heard more than his fair share of prospector stories and had a few stock certificates given to him in payment for medical services. None had ever panned out. Just the same, I was surprised to witness his outburst of profanity, which also shocked Ebbie. I guess seeing his retirement plans going up in smoke only added to his frustration.

After several days of grumbling, we sat down one night after supper to consider what Dad was going to do. Before the Doc could open his mouth, Ebbie looked at both of us and offered: "Doctor Lawson, I've run your household for over ten years and I have something to say about Tom asking for money. I know you're upset over not hearing from Tom all those years, but he's always been a good boy—er, I guess a man by now. So now he comes up with asking for a loan and you're reacting like a wounded bull. Tell me, where else should you be investing your money? It's no different than providing money for Ben here becoming a doctor. Sure, much bigger risk, but an investment all the same. Tell you what, Doctor Lawson. I've been saving for the day you retire and if you don't want to help Tom out, then by golly, I will." With that, Ebbie got up from the table and shuffled down the hall to her room. We were both speechless.

I don't think either one of us believed that Ebbie had five thousand dollars, but that wasn't the point. It didn't take Dad but a day or so to tell us that he was going to loan Tom the money and agree to my going to Arizona to be with my brother for a year. Ebbie just smiled and went about her business as usual. Dad's last words were, "Yes, Ben, but only for a year."

So, in the fall of 1863, I left Denver to journey to El Paso, Texas. I had five hundred dollars sewed inside my jacket and a bank draft for forty-five hundred dollars buried in my medical kit wrapped in a roll of bandage. The ride from Denver took me south and parallel to the Rocky Mountains, rising majestically in Colorado and New Mexico. I enjoyed a brief layover in Santa Fe, slept past Albuquerque, finally arriving in the border town of El Paso after three days of tortuous sitting. Spanish was the most spoken language in El Paso, but I had no problem making myself understood, particularly in the Mexican restaurants.

When the stage driver shouted for us to climb on board, I grabbed a corner seat, pulled my hat down over my eyes, and went to sleep, with my medical bag at my feet. In spite of the bumpy ride and periodic shouts of the stage driver, I managed to stay drowsy enough to completely ignore my fellow riders.

KATE HURLEY

Wayne County, Tennessee, a rural community of good farmland and hard wood timber, lies one hundred miles east of Memphis. It was located in the south-central part of the state, and farmers produced grain, fruits and vegetables and raised cows, pigs and sheep. Before the Civil War, families lived uncomplicated, prosperous lives. Tennessee was a slave state supporting the Confederacy, and contributed heavily to the cause, in manpower, horses, and foodstuff.

Dave Hurley's spread was larger than most; he raised horses, cut timber and grew corn, wheat, barley, oats and vegetables. Dave ran the farm with the help of his wife Doris, daughter Kate and two Negro slave families. Son Joe had volunteered for service at the beginning of the war and was a cavalry officer stationed in western Virginia. Letters from Joe were few and far between. In spite of a general labor shortage, southern Tennessee continued to prosper during the war with Lincoln and the Union.

At sixteen, Kate Hurley had completed home schooling in reading, writing and arithmetic and had taken over the financial management of the Hurley farm. Dad preferred outdoor work, Mom had no interest or skill in tallying up figures and Joe was away fighting in the war. While she had little choice in the matter, Kate managed the books and got quite proficient in negotiating contracts. Local bankers and traders soon recognized her skills and learned to respect her common sense approach to business matters. In fact, after dealing with Kate, traders voiced preference for working with the less demanding Dave Hurley. She was also an accomplished rider and could handle cattle as well as her Dad and brother. Mom Hurley often thanked the good Lord that the Confederacy refused to consider women for military service, excepting nursing. She could easily see her only daughter dashing between military posts evading the enemy as a courier.

Concerned that Kate was spending too much time with the slave families, teaching their children to read and write, the Hurleys sent her to finishing school in Petersburg, Virginia. While at the academy, she developed a strong distaste for slavery, which did not sit well with the school's headmistress. Shortly before graduation, she debated the slavery issue with an instructor, who reported her unpatriotic remarks to Miss Pottinger. The altercation prompted the school to demand Miss Hurley's withdrawal from the school to pre-empt an expulsion order. Dave Hurley did not enjoy the letter which explained treasonable behavior and the unforgiving, unladylike demeanor of his daughter. Miss Pottinger breathed a sigh of relief when Kate withdrew from school and boarded the train for Nashville.

Dave Hurley met his daughter in the state's capitol, where he immediately questioned Kate's early departure from the exclusive finishing school for young ladies. "Daughter, I spent a lot of money to send you to Miss Pottinger's, and I don't appreciate you getting kicked out because you can't keep your smart remarks to yourself. Since when did you become an expert on how to handle darkies? I've had Negro slaves working for me for over twenty years and I don't need you or anyone else telling me how I should handle 'em. Ezekiel and Jonah were bought and paid for a long time ago and wouldn't know any other way of life. One of these days you'll learn to keep your mouth quiet when wiser adults are speaking to you, trying to get you educated. Jonah and Ezekiel can read and write, but they're the exception. Most of those people are only good for field work."

At first Kate refused to respond, so her Dad droned on. "Slaves have been here for over 200 years and without them we couldn't grow and harvest the cotton necessary for export to support the war. Your brother is up north somewhere fighting to preserve our way of life and you've been alienating fellow students and teachers. It's insane and not the way you were brought up."

Finally, with tears in her eyes, Kate glared at her father and said, "Daddy, this is 1863 and the war is taking a terrible toll on the people of Virginia. Food is being rationed, hospitals are full of wounded and maimed young men and all you can preach is loyalty to the Confederacy. Slavery is morally wrong and in due time, Jeff Davis will have to quit, because the Yankees have more people to call on, more industry and the willingness to preserve the Union. Eventually, people like you will have to face the fact that black people can't be treated like animals. I've talked to people who have been in the North and read newspapers from Boston and New York. They want to free the slaves and will do whatever it takes to make it happen. Just wait, you'll see."

In the next few days, father and daughter barely talked to one another and avoided any further conversation on the issue of slavery. Dave Hurley was deeply disturbed however. As they drifted down the Tennessee River, he began to recognize how much his daughter had changed in the past few years. She'd always been concerned for the health and welfare of the slave Negro families, but now she'd turned into a Northern sympathizer. While he didn't like it or agree with her position, he had to accept that right or wrong, Kate Hurley had grown up and had a mind of her own. "Where," he thought, "is this going to take us and how can I get things back to where they used to be?" Sadly, he concluded that things would never be the same again.

The forty-mile buggy ride from Peter's Landing to the farm was traveled in virtual silence. Ezekiel cracked the whip once or twice to pick up the pace; Kate devoured the familiar landscape as they clip-clopped over the well-worn dirt road. The closer the trio got to the homestead, the more Kate appreciated the progress that her father had made with the farm in her absence.

In the yard at the house, Kate jumped down from the rig and rushed to her mother's arms in a shower of tears. Mrs. Hurley hugged her daughter, silently sensing that father and daughter were at odds, thinking the issue was related to Kate's departure from school. After a cup of tea, Kate toured the new barns and corrals, reaching for something that would restore peace in the family. Unfortunately, her reunion with Ezekiel and Jonah and their families only reminded her of the gulf between her and her father. When she rejoined her parents, she saw that her Mom had been crying, undoubtedly over Kate's rebuke of slavery, lack of patriotism for the Confederacy and arguing with her Dad.

Over a dinner of ham, squash and cornbread, the family enjoyed a brief interlude of peace and quiet. The controversy over slavery was carefully avoided, but Doris Hurley knew that relations between father and daughter were seriously strained; they were too much alike in their habits and actions not to be noticed.

Most of the time, Kate busied herself with the horses or took long, solitary rides with her favorite mare. It was on one of these excursions that Kate realized that she was not a member of the Southern elite who survived and prospered on the labors of the Negro slave population. Farming or ranching in Tennessee was not going to be her cup of tea and it was time that she began to explore other options. In the process, she became closer to her mother, who seemed to understand the dilemma she was confronted with. Loving her Mom and Dad and settling down with one of the local farm boys to raise a family just wasn't going to be enough for Miss Kate.

One morning, after another restless night of thinking about her future, she let her mind wander away from the war, slavery and the confederacy, which, she was convinced, was going to be eventually defeated. The North had more resources and the naval blockade was restricting the South's ability to export cotton to finance the war. Kate suggested to her mother that they ride out to Grapeleaf Falls, a secluded spot neither of them had visited in several years. Surprised, but sensing that her daughter wanted to talk, Doris Hurley donned jeans, a blouse and a wide-brimmed cowboy hat in ready agreement. They packed a picnic lunch of beef jerky, cornbread and fruit and quietly left the ranch house. Dan Hurley watched and wondered as they trotted away from home. "Well, that sure is nice to see Mom and Kate off by themselves for a ride. Maybe Doris will be able to talk some sense into that kid's head."

Grapeleaf Falls was a secluded spot where a spring-fed stream flowed over an escarpment, creating a waterfall of about twelve feet. At the base of the falls, there was a shallow pond, eroded out of sandstone by water many thousands of years ago. The natural depression created an ideal place of seclusion. It was one of Kate's childhood hideaways, where she and her brother often escaped to. The pool and waterfall were framed by a tumble of thick vines, grape leaves and fruit.

Tying their horses to a tree branch, the Hurleys took off their boots to dip their feet into the chilly water. Doris Hurley waited patiently for her daughter to open the conversation. "Mom, I know the past few weeks have been very hard on you, and not the homecoming you'd hoped for. My inability to express myself to you has only made things worse. I expect that Dad has given you the details of our talks on the way home from Nashville, so I won't dwell on them, unless you want my side of the disagreement.

"The reason I wanted to be alone with you is to talk with you, quietly, without any interruptions from Dad. The Confederacy will lose this war and the period following their defeat will be difficult for the plantation owners, farmers and ranchers, like you and Dad. I think you'll survive okay, as I'm guessing that Jonah and Ezekiel and their families will stay on as free men. Your ranch and farm is also home to them and they will not be moving on like many of the blacks.

"Much as I love you both, I just don't see myself settling down here. I can't think of any local boy I'd be willing to spend the rest of my life with to farm and raise a family. Maybe I'll never have a family. I hope and pray my brother comes home in one piece, to enjoy a new life centered around the ranch and you folks. If all this sounds pretty selfish on my part, I'll admit that it probably is, and for that, I'm sorry."

Doris Hurley was not surprised or taken aback by her daughter's confession. She loved her daughter deeply and hoped that she would settle down on the farm, marry and raise children, as she had, but knew that Kate was far more ambitious and self-confident. She also recognized that she was more of an explorer, comfortable with new faces and anxious to travel to new places. She had no idea where these attributes came from or where they would lead, but was confident it would work out well for her. Still, she hoped that Kate wouldn't move North and end up marrying a Yankee.

"Kate, there's no need to apologize. I've known for some time that you were a strong, independent young lady, destined for far more than being a farmer's wife in the state of Tennessee. You've got a lot of your father's individuality, a trait that will be hard for any man to contain.

"I suspect you're probably right about the Union and Lincoln winning this war; my greatest concern is getting my son back home safe and sound. I'm worn out worrying about the shooting, killing and wounding of so many people, Blue and Gray. We haven't heard a word from your brother in over two months and it's about to drive me crazy. If we're running the war like our postal service, we're in serious trouble, and I think we are. I can see your Dad beginning to give up on Jefferson Davis. I don't worry too much about freeing the slaves, at least on our place. They've been with us for over twenty years, shared in our joys and sorrows, and are part of our family. I agree with you, I believe they will stay put with us, at least until their boys are grown up."

While Doris Hurley took a break and sipped her tea, Kate looked at her Mom in genuine surprise. This wife of a Tennessee rancher obviously had thoughts about a lot of things that she'd kept quiet about all these years. It gave Kate a new, warm feeling towards her mother. And, her mother wasn't finished.

"Kate, several months ago I received a letter from your Aunt Barbara, your father's sister. She lives in the New Mexico Territory, going there after her army husband was killed in a battle with Apache Indians. Some refer to the area as Arizona and New Mexico, but the map I looked at said New Mexico Territory. Anyway, it's a huge expanse of rugged mountains and desert and very few people. She lives in a small town called Ribera and works in a general store, from what she said. If it helps any, Ribera is somewhere between El Paso and Tucson. The years have gone by quickly and her son, following in his father's footsteps, is now a senior cadet at West Point Military Academy. She seems to have done very well for herself as she now owns the store. I'll get the letter so you can read it for yourself and maybe you can drop her a note. I always liked Aunt Barbara but Dad always felt that she was a little too independent for her own good. He thought she was off her rocker when she decided to marry an army man and go West."

"Mom, I don't know what to say; you amaze me at times. I was giving some thought to California and now you come up with Aunt Barbara in Arizona. That could make more sense as it would get me out West, but with an aunt that could maybe provide me with a start. And, connecting with a relative would give you and Dad peace of mind, knowing where I was." Excitedly, Kate hugged her Mom and shouted, "I love you!"

They took their time returning to the ranch, enjoying the sunset as they rode up to the main house. Dave Hurley was pleased to see the looks on Doris and Kate as they entered the house, but decided to leave their smiling faces be. Over supper, Dave became suspicious when Aunt Barbara's name entered the conversation, but decided not to ask questions, at least for the moment. He did get the feeling though that he was missing out on some new developments, between mother and daughter. He figured he'd learn about it soon enough.

When he was advised of Kate's possible relocation to Arizona, his aspirations for his daughter were turned upside down. He was also very unhappy with his wife, who he felt was co-conspirator in the plot.

During the following week, a letter made up and signed by Mrs. Hurley and Kate was sent off to the New Mexico Territory, addressed to Aunt Barbara. Several weeks went by without a word from the West. Then Kate received a lengthy letter from "Mrs. Barbara Casey" that reopened her idea of leaving Tennessee. She shared its contents with Mom and Dad, who said little as Kate read the message out loud. Thoughtfully, Kate decided to allow her parents some thinking time as she withdrew from the kitchen. In the quiet of her bedroom, Kate re-read the letter and immediately decided to accept her aunt's invitation to spend a few months in Ribera with her, in the fall. The weather would be much better, and Aunt Barbara would be given some time to fix up a room for her niece. She also wanted to avoid the triple-digit temperatures and rainy season of the Southwest. Throughout the letter, her aunt was enthusiastic over the possible visit by Kate to see her.

Kate's mother knew that her daughter was going to accept Aunt Barbara's invitation, even before the invitation arrived. She worried about Kate's safety, but trusted Barbara Casey's judgment to do the right thing and protect her daughter in this new venture. At the same time, she had little knowledge of the town she was going to visit, the people and the threat of Indian warfare. There was simply very little news available on that part of the country. As she helped Kate pack for the trip, Doris Hurley also prayed for her daughter's safety.

Dave Hurley was clearly shaken when Kate announced her intention of leaving Tennessee for the "wild West," as he saw it. He could not believe she would make this decision without his counsel and permission. As a consequence, he was hurt, mad and upset.

Gradually, though, he realized that Kate had made up her mind and was definitely leaving. He would have to accept her decision or risk losing her forever. One lazy afternoon, when both were sitting on a corral rail, he turned to his daughter and said, "Kate, I'm sorry this has turned out this way, but I want you to know that I love you and want nothing but the best for you. If things don't work out for you with Aunt Barbara, come on home. Take care of yourself and please write, and keep in touch with your Mom. Your leaving home will be hard on her." Kate could only nod in agreement before her eyes filled with tears.

Kate's departure from her Mom was equally difficult; neither could find the right words to say goodbye. Finally, Doris Hurley looked at her daughter, with tears streaming down her cheeks and said, "Honey, be good to yourself, give my best to Aunt Barbara, and remember, this will always be your home. Your room will be untouched by anyone until you come back to visit or stay. Good luck; I love you." While shorter, her goodbyes to the families of Jonah and Ezekiel were equally tense.

BART LaGRANGE

"You better listen up and get your ass back in that ditch. You'll get water when I decide to give it to you, and not before. You think this is some kind of a fancy hotel?"

Corporal Josh Bettencourt then lashed Bart LaGrange across his shoulder with a thick, fire-hardened wooden staff, the blow sending the prisoner headlong into the irrigation canal. "Get up and get back to work or you'll be in the black box for a week!" Bart staggered to his feet, picked up his shovel and painfully returned to his digging. He had no desire to spend a week in solitary confinement, on bread and water, where temperatures went over 110 degrees. Once in the steel box was enough to get anybody's attention.

During his three months in the West Texas prison, Bart learned that a ten-year confinement was really a death sentence. The inmates were worked at hard labor ten hours a day, the food was poor and water rations inadequate. The guards, who hated the remote prison as much as the inmates, brutalized the prisoners on a regular basis. Conversation with other inmates convinced Bart that he wouldn't live out his sentence, nor would he see his sentence reduced for good behavior. Bribery was common to get preferential treatment, but without a source of money, that option was not available to him. In short, he had to figure out a way to get out of the prison, or perish, and time was running out.

The late spring cloudburst took everyone by surprise. The sky rapidly blackened, the wind picked up and rain and hailstones ripped through the bivouac. The guards ran for protection in their shanties, ignoring the fate of the prisoners.

Hailstones two inches in diameter pounded the tin roofs of the shanties and the bare-backed prisoners, who sought refuge lying in their dry canals.

In the ensuing confusion, protected by darkness, LaGrange decided that this was the best opportunity for escape he might ever get. The darkness covered the prisoners in a black shroud while the guards decided to stay in their own safe place. Shackled at the ankles, Bart pushed and shoved his way down the ditch to where it stopped. He then stood up to get his bearings, heard the rushing water, and ran, stumbled and picked himself up like a man in a three-legged race. When he reached the bank of the river, he barely saw the outline of a large tree, floating rapidly downstream. Without hesitation, he jumped into the swirling mass of water, reaching out for a limb to attach himself to. It took all his strength to hold onto the tree as it bumped and twisted in the gushing stream of boiling water. Welded to the tree, Bart was swept several miles from the prison camp where the current finally deposited him in a mass of debris in a shallow inlet.

He lay shivering on the narrow beach for several hours, totally exhausted from the ordeal. Finally, he inched his way into a thicket of mesquite, where he fell asleep. Just before dawn he was awakened by a herd of javelinas, grousing for food near the mesquite bushes. He lay quietly, rubbing his hands and legs to regain some circulation. As the sun began to rise, though, he realized that he had to keep moving west, away from the prison, where surely his absence would be noted at morning call.

As the sun lit up the day, Bart collected himself and drew a mental map of where he believed he was and where he had to go. He was tired, hungry, without a weapon, but also determined to complete his escape. Moving due west, he was surprised that he didn't hear any dogs barking; he hoped the guards reported him missing and assumed dead from drowning. Maybe he'd get lucky for a change; he knew that penalties were severe for guards that allowed a prisoner to escape. He also recognized, though, that it was more likely that he was being sought by bloodhounds and armed guards. He moved on.

With the sun warming his back and drying his clothes, he followed a faint trail that took him to an abandoned group of buildings that had seen better days as a stage stop or a remote shanty used at roundup times. His search for food ended with the discovery of a tin of peaches. Continuing his exploration, Bart found blacksmith tools that enabled him to open the can of peaches and work on the removal of his leg irons. He chipped away at the leg irons for most of the day, finally succeeding to remove his last identification as a Texas state prisoner. He was elated with this accomplishment; he was now a free man. Nevertheless, goaded by the prospect of recapture, he pushed on, determined to get away from any posse on his trail and to reach Old Mexico.

Bart LaGrange was the bastard son of Carl LaGrange and Molly Simpson, his barmaid mistress. Within six weeks of his birth, the baby Bart was shuffled off to a spinster aunt, who worked as a laundress in Cairo, Illinois. Bart never saw his parents again, and in later life had no recollection of what they looked like, or why they had abandoned him to Aunt Flora.

Aunt Flora doted on the boy and did her best to raise him in a Christian manner. She also saw that the boy received home schooling in reading, writing and arithmetic. At an early age, though, young Bart drifted to the river and the hustle bustle of paddle wheelers loading and unloading freight and passengers. He loved the activity of the Mississippi waterfront and soon learned the art of pickpocketing, storing his loot beneath a floorboard in the small room where he lived with his aunt. Blinded by matronly love, Aunt Flora never suspected that her ward had graduated into petty thievery, and pretty successfully.

Bart was twelve years old when Aunt Flora contracted pneumonia and died. Faced with the prospect of eviction and being sent to an orphanage, the young man retrieved his pickpocket holdings and became a stowaway on the Ohio Queen, which stopped regularly in Cairo on its southward journey to New Orleans. At first, he was able to keep well hidden, but eventually was caught by the head cook while stealing food from the galley. The cook turned the youngster over to the second mate, who, without asking any questions, beat up the youngster severely. Rusty Bagley was a large, rough-cut sailor who enjoyed thrashing young roustabouts and people looking for a free ride. Most times he took their money and forced them to pay their passage by working in the kitchen or casino room.

Bart was no exception. Threatened with being tossed overboard, Bart coughed up his savings to the mate and found himself in the gambling casino as a janitor. Here, he quickly adjusted to the new conditions and took on a new, exciting education. Under the tutelage of Jake, the head bartender, he became an expert student of gambling and prostitution.

The gaming room of the Ohio Queen was large and always crowded with men and women gamblers anxious to win. Bart had plenty to do mopping floors, sometimes serving drinks and generally soliciting tips. People liked the young man and with the endorsement of Jake and the mate, Bart thrived. He was accepted by dealers, waitresses and the entertainers and learned to service the heavy hitters with whatever they wanted. By carefully observing the dealers, the rigged roulette wheel and the servers, he became acclimated and prospered. A couple of the bar maids also assisted in his learning more about women than he should have at his age. Then again he was close to full manhood and such was life on the Mississippi in the mid 1800's. By the age of fourteen, Bart could deal a fair hand of stud poker and knew that beds were not exclusively for sleeping. He also learned to placate the second mate; a smart move, in view of Rusty's well-earned reputation for intolerance and violence.

In his third year on board the Ohio Queen, Bart abandoned the boat to begin a new life in New Orleans. He had clothes, some money in his pocket, and was ready for a new adventure.

He checked into the Parisian Hotel, a moderately priced establishment that would provide excellent temporary housing while Bart learned the lay of the city. It was at the Shamrock Hotel a few days later that Bart met Duke Kirkwood, a notorious gambler and part-time bank robber. Bested at the poker table by the youngster, the gambler invited Bart to the lounge to share a drink. "Son, I like the way you handle yourself with the cards. I won't question whether it's pure luck or skill, but let's join up together for a few days and see if we can make some real money."

For the next week, the twosome had an unusually good streak of face cards and managed to sock away over a thousand dollars apiece, without mishap. Bart was elated that he'd come into such good luck. Unknown to him, though, Duke Kirkwood had recently robbed several banks in Kansas and had killed a teller in East Texas. He was also a shrewd judge of character and saw Bart the newcomer as a new way to expand his operations. With training, this fresh face would become the gang's new lookout for evaluating potential bank robberies. Bart was unknown in the area, was intelligent and ambitious and could learn how to "case" a targeted bank.

"Bart, we've had some fun and made a good haul here in New Orleans, but it's time to move on. You've also convinced me that you're ready for a bigger challenge. Me and my friends have some work to do in East Texas and we'd like you to join up with us. It's a little risky, but it's a good way to make some quick, big money. You won't be involved with the heavy stuff, we just need you to scout out a few banks and we'll handle the rest. Are you interested?"

Young Bart LaGrange knew that the offer was shady, but was fascinated with the new adventure, and besides, felt that Duke was a good guy. He rationalized that it might involve some sort of a swindle but surely, no serious gunplay. When he was formally introduced to the Kirkwood gang, he realized that he was in over his head with no way out. Their mood, manner and conversation soon convinced him that they were a group of professional hoodlums who robbed and killed for a living. He also knew that there was little chance of his walking away from the gang, at least at this time. He would have to bide his time until an escape opportunity arose. For the near future, he'd have to make the best of the situation and play along with Duke, who, suddenly, had become all business.

In spite of earlier promises, Duke insisted that Bart learn how to handle a pistol and shotgun. Day after day, he practiced shooting with a brand new Colt .44, 1860 model, until Duke was satisfied with his marksmanship. He also learned to draw and shoot, until his hand quivered with fatigue. The shotgun was much easier to handle. Finally, Duke took Bart aside and advised, "Kid, never point your pistol at anyone unless you intend to shoot to kill. It's not likely that you'll ever get close to a fire fight, but you need to be handy with your gun for self-defense. You've learned well; let's hope that all goes well for both of us."

Six months of drinking, hiding, gambling and whoring had left the gang broke, edgy and ready to resume their regular habits. When Duke called the gang members together, they were anxious for instructions and ready to do battle. Gathering in the hills near the Red River of east Texas, they discussed how to scout Bowie and Cass counties for the best holdup opportunities. It was clear to Bart LaGrange that the gang was well led and experienced in hitting banks that many times were poorly secured.

Unfortunately for the Kirkwood gang, a few things had changed in the past six months. The highjacking exploits of the Kirkwood gang had drawn the attention of senior Wells Fargo officials, who realized that the gang had to be stopped. Between stage coach robberies and bank heists, the public was losing confidence in the company and jeopardizing deposits. With this new commitment, police and security officials fanned out across Texas and Kansas, seeking the whereabouts of Duke Kirkwood and his band of cutthroats. Rewards were posted, informers contacted in hopes of gaining access to where the gang was in hiding. They knew things had been quiet for too long, but still they came up with nothing. Where would the Duke hit next? Would it be the stage run between Joplin, Missouri, and Texarkana, Arkansas, or would they swarm over the rural communities? At long last, they received a lead from a peace officer who was sure he'd spotted a stranger looking a little too carefully at a bank in Creosote, Texas. Detectives were excited; this could be the break they were looking for.

Bart had received extensive training from Duke personally on how to reconnoiter a bank. One had to dress properly as a potential customer, use multiple disguises and be as inconspicious as possible, being on the lookout at all times. Then there was the bank itself, the busy and quiet times, access and escape routes, manufacturer of the safe and overall security.

Entering the county seat of Creosote, Texas, Bart rode into town wearing a moustache, glasses, and a business suit. As he tied his mount to the hotel hitching post, he coolly looked up and down Main Street, searching for a vantage point where he could observe town traffic. He finally decided on a window seat at the Willows Hotel dining room and ordered a plate of food. After the meal of steak and beans, he watched the bank in operation. Overall, it looked pretty routine to him, including a brief visit to the bank. He was confident that he'd done his job well and could give Duke a positive, full report. Even the small deposit he made seemed to be pretty routine. The bank president was eager to explain how well the bank was protected from any robbery attempt. On his way out of town, a Wells Fargo detective had luckily detected Bart's more than casual interest in the bank, and had shadowed Bart on his tour of the town. He'd even sat close by in the hotel dining room as Bart took mental notes of the bank visitors.

When the Kirkwood gang rode into town a few days later, from opposite ends of town, the local sheriff and Wells Fargo agents were well prepared to meet the thieves. Being the first of the gang to enter the bank probably saved Bart LaGrange's life. When Duke Kirkwood and Sam Shorter pulled pistols and yelled "Hands up!" they were met with a barrage of gunfire that killed both men and wounded Bart as he attempted to escape. The armed "tellers" had completely surprised the robbers and quelled the attempt to crack the only bank in town. For once, the good guys had something to talk about.

Two other gang members, guarding getaway points, were also shot and killed in the melee. Only one quick-thinking thug, though wounded, managed to escape the ambush. As he tore out of town, he saw LaGrange standing near the sheriff, and thought that maybe he was in on the entrapment. He became convinced, as he rode away, that the slaughter was somehow connected to the gang's newest recruit. Someday, somewhere, he'd get even with that son of a bitch if it was the last thing in the world he'd get to do. That is, if he were able to make his own escape. He jammed his spurs into the stallion to accelerate his ride to safety.

Bart LaGrange had Lady Luck on his side, again. While slightly wounded, he was captured by the sheriff's deputy and brought to a speedy trial. During the court proceedings, he was able to convince the jury that he had only recently joined the Kirkwood gang—under duress—and had no connection with Duke's previous killings and robberies. He breathed easier when the judge sentenced him to ten years hard labor in prison at Fort Stockton, Texas. That feeling would change quickly after a few weeks in the desert, breaking rocks and digging ditches.

It took Bart the better part of a month to reach the Rio Grande River and cross into Chihuahua, Mexico. He'd been befriended by a wagon master leading a group of settlers to El Paso, who had saved him from death from starvation and heat stroke. Had he not been found by the wagon train, he would surely have perished in the Texas desert. The last week of his adventure, he'd left the wagon master and hiked over the Devil Ridge Eagle Mountain with a hand-drawn map given to him by the man.

Now, below the border, Bart was again confronted with the problem of no food and no money. He hoped that knowing a few words of prison Spanish would help him elude any bounty hunters and help him find food. Entering a cantina, he saw two American cowboys busy talking over shot glasses of tequila at a table. The taller of the two lifted his hand slightly and offered Bart a drink. "Stranger, you look like you've been through a war. Come on over and join us in a drink; you may just be the guy we're looking for."

Barely able to stand, Bart sat down, chugged the shot of tequila, promptly passed out and slipped to the dirt floor of the bar. When he awoke, he was in a crib usually reserved for prostitutes and their customers. However, it was quiet, he was alone and light shining through a window told him it was morning. He heard a gentle knock on the door and an elderly senora entered the room asking if he were hungry. He replied, "Si, gracias." She soon returned with a steaming platter of native enchiladas and beans, which he rapidly devoured. She provided him with a second helping of refried beans, which he washed down with a hot cup of chicory flavored Mexican coffee.

Moments later, he was joined by the two cowboys that he had met on the previous day. "Stranger, we don't know who you are, but can guess where you've been; those leg iron scars are a dead giveaway. Now you don't have to worry about us, we're not lawmen or bounty hunters. We're Bill and Jack Stinson and we need help getting a train of horses to Fort Bliss, Texas. We bought 'em down here from the Pantero family; they were supposed to give us a couple of vaqueros to help us get the horses to the Army, but the old man is sick and the boys won't leave the ranch. We'll pay you well to help us get these nags north, no questions asked."

Bart only smiled and nodded his assent. "Good, there's a store near the Mercado where you can get riding gear for our account. Don't forget to get two canteens; water's scarce the way we're going. Here's some money for personal stuff; tell Miguel we'll be down later to settle with him. Get all the rest you can; we'll be leaving in the morning. If you need us for anything, we'll be at Miguel's house around the corner from the store. We'll see you at the livery stable at sunup, tomorrow morning. We've already taken care of a good mount and saddle for you. If you have other needs beyond food and drink, Conchita at the cantina will be able to help you out. Just don't drink too much; we've got a long day ahead of us tomorrow."

At dawn the following morning, Bart walked to the edge of town and the livery stable. Bill and Jack Stinson waved good morning as Bart was given his horse, already saddled. With the addition of Juan, an older Mexican, the riders started the drive to El Paso and Fort Bliss, Texas. A week later, Bart thanked the Stinsons for all their help and said goodbye to the brothers. He didn't want to press his luck by entering a U.S. Army post. Their gift of the horse and saddle gave him renewed hope for a new and better beginning.

PETER HILLENBRAND

Winthrop and Eleanor Hillenbrand landed in New York harbor in 1772 after a stormy winter crossing of the Atlantic. They'd decided to leave England when the royal family began persecuting people who would not adhere to strict Anglican Church doctrine. They had abandoned most of their business property, leaving with other Quakers, with very little material possessions. They settled in New York, where Winthrop established himself as a maritime trader, specializing in foodstuffs, spices, clothing and hand tools. Through hard work and smart, but honest, trading, he rapidly built a prosperous business and a first-rate reputation.

Just prior to the start of the American Revolution, Winthrop Hillenbrand moved his wife and family to the city of Philadelphia where he quickly established himself again as an astute trader and supporter of the revolt against England. When he died suddenly in 1810, his only son took over the family business and grew the trade volume twice over, supporting the Federal government during the War of 1812.

When Peter Hillenbrand was born in 1840, he instantly became part of Philadelphia's elite society. He attended boarding school in Connecticut and graduated from the College of New Jersey, which is today's Princeton University. Active on campus at the College of New Jersey in sports, he also managed to graduate with honors in the Romance Languages. Two summers were spent in Paris and Rome, where the young man practiced spoken French and Italian, chasing local debutantes.

After college, Peter joined the investment banking firm of Batchelder, Monroni and Gable in lower Manhattan, apprenticing for eventual work with his father's firm. BM&G, as it was popularly known, was well regarded for its support of President Lincoln and its ability to procure and deliver war materials for the Union Army. Well connected in the New England states, they were particularly successful in contracting for guns, ammunition and explosives and having them delivered when they were vitally needed. In the process, massive fortunes were built for the partners. None of the BM & G executives, key employees or close relatives never came close to serving in the Union Army. They simply substituted hired Irish, Italian and German immigrants to take their place to comply with government conscription regulations. Peter Hillenbrand was no exception; the closest he got to the war was what he read in the paper and bar room talk in the financial district of the city. His thoughts were more attuned to keeping his creditors at bay and avoiding family questions on just what he did in his spare time, if he had any. He and his father quarreled regularly on why Peter was not getting promoted in the firm of BM&G.

As the war began to show serious signs of defeat for the Confederacy, the alert directors of the firm looked westward to Texas and California and whatever lay in between. Well connected in Washington, they knew that the administration would invest heavily to build infrastructure to connect the West Coast with the more populated Eastern seaboard. Knowing that the federal government was going to subsidize population growth in the Southwest, the partners wanted to be in the forefront of these developments. While early in the game, they knew that eventually, railroads and the telegraph would link both coasts. They also knew that Western gold and silver strikes like the Comstock Lode in Nevada were going to provide all kinds of investment opportunity. They were especially interested in establishing some sort of distribution network to peddle manufactured goods made in New England, where they enjoyed solid relations with producers of hardware, hand tools, clocks and various household goods. Setting up a supply system to sell these products to farmers, miners and ranchers seemed to offer interesting possibilities. Maybe the time was ripe to send someone out to explore the area before every competitor came to the same conclusion.

For several reasons, Peter Hillenbrand, or "PH" as he was known within the firm, became the candidate to look over the firm's interests in the great Southwest.

Hostilities in Texas had died down, so they weren't putting Peter's life in jeopardy. With a little luck, the war might even be over before Peter arrived in Texas. While Peter was generally well liked within the firm, he annoyed his superiors by flouting company rules. He dated several female employees, was usually late for work on Monday mornings and was always complaining that he wasn't making enough money to support his lifestyle. The problem was compounded by Peter's father, who was always asking how his son was doing and why he hadn't been promoted. In fact, if Peter's father had not been an important client of the firm, young Peter would have been discharged long ago. At the same time, "PH" was well informed, bright and anxious to take on new responsibilities. Perhaps this was the opportunity to solve several problems for the partners. When he heard that the firm was going to explore the Southwest, Peter was intrigued and dove into researching the geography, culture and gross national production of the states and territories. It was a mammoth undertaking for such a short period, but "PH" virtually moved into the local library and went to work, preparing for a possible interview for the job.

When Peter was called into the office of a senior partner, he was well prepared to discuss the situation on equal or better terms than the interviewer. He'd read the history of Spanish and Mexican occupation, knew the geography and physiology of the Southwest and had examined the Gadsden Purchase and Mexican war documents. His knowledge of the Spanish language also gave him added insight into the habits and religious customs of the vast territories. When Mr. Batchelder invited Peter out to lunch, he knew he had a good chance to win the position.

Old man Batchelder reviewed cattle ranching, the mining of gold and silver and the imminent flood of people that would surely create huge economic opportunities for the firm and for "PH." The more Peter listened, the more he felt that it really was a way to explore new possibilities. When the partner told him he would receive a substantial raise and an expense account, the deal was closed.

When Peter asked how long the project would take, and what would be involved, Batchelder replied, "Peter, we expect that you'll be in the West for twelve to eighteen months. We also want you to take a look at the business climate in northern Mexico, where a lot of silver mining is going on. The real plum is probably southern California, but we want you to travel through the New Mexico Territory where stage lines are being opened, and eventually we'll see railroads. God, I wish I were your age; I'd want to be going myself. I'm sure your Dad will be thrilled to know that you've decided to be the company's point man on a project of this importance. I wish you good luck, Peter, and remember, you're always representing the firm. Finally, some fatherly advice: Watch yourself with the ladies and control yourself when it comes to drinking, particularly with strangers."

Peter was surprised with Batchelder's "fatherly advice" remarks, but only smiled to himself and decided to let it go. Later in the day, though, he pondered, "Jesus, I wonder if the ole buzzard knows anything about Colleen."

"PH" had a very active social life in New York, from debutantes with family connections to every imaginable lesser privileged female. He frequented lower East Side saloons as easily and as frequently as snooty coming out parties for the city's upper crust. He kept himself so busy partying that he rarely went home for a weekend in Philadelphia. "Why would I want to sit around listening to Dad expound about the stock market or answer Mom's relentless questioning about New York society?"

His involvement with Colleen O'Hara couldn't be ignored or dismissed as easily. He'd met Colleen in a gin mill, where she worked as a waitress. Before long, he had rented a flat for the girl, where they set up housekeeping. He didn't love her, but thoroughly enjoyed her bedroom manners, believing he could break up the romance any time he wanted to.

A week ago, she'd confided to him that she was pregnant and expected him to marry her before a Catholic priest. As their sensuous relationship came crashing to a halt, Peter realized the girl was serious and wanted him as a husband. Peter searched for all kinds of a solution, to no avail. She was insulted at the thought of an abortion or an orphanage. The thought of a confrontation with Paddy O'Hara, Colleen's father, chilled him to the bone. With the company offer to leave New York and be away for an extended period, "PH" decided to run away from the problem, like a true member of New York high society.

Peter met with Benson Appleby, company office manager, to arrange travel to Texas and stations west. Lines of credit were established, transportation options explored, and periodic reports agreed to, so the partners would be aware of Peter's whereabouts. After satisfying Appleby's instructions, boring as they were, Peter dashed back to his flat, knowing that Colleen would still be at work at the Shamrock Saloon. When he reached the flat, he quickly packed all his personal belongings, destroyed all evidence of where he worked, and departed for the Battery. Here, he located the Galveston Clipper, the ship he was due to leave on in a few days. The purser was surprised at his early arrival, but with a first class reservation, saw that his passenger was well taken care of. Peter's cabin was spartan by any standards, but felt like the Ritz to a man escaping the clutches of a pregnant girlfriend. As he looked out the porthole of the ship, lights beckoned "PH" ashore for a fine dinner, wine, and "who knows what else?" Suddenly, life was good again.

The sail from New York around Florida and across the Gulf of Mexico was uneventful, but blazing hot and humid most of the time. The only other passengers were a family visiting New Orleans and of little interest to Peter. At times, he dined with the captain, a sour old retired whaler who was only interested in the weather and arriving in port on time. When the Galveston Clipper reached the Texas coast, Peter gathered his belongings, anxious to be on land again, and disembarked. The last segment of the trip to El Paso was over 750 miles and he wanted to get there as quickly as possible. As the stagecoach left the port of Galveston, the driver shouted, "First stop, Austin!"

As the stage bumped and groaned over the dusty, windy road, Peter wondered why old Appleby hadn't put him on board a ship for San Diego or Los Angeles. This part of the country seemed like a wasteland, seldom broken by a sole cow or wrangler working a fenceline. Even the people in Galveston thought he was crazy to leave the port city for the interior and El Paso. "Hell, Mister, you're still in Mexico goin' to that cow town. You'll see, there ain't nothin' there but run-down buildings and a slew of people lookin' for work."

It took over a week and a broken axle to reach the border city. Even after checking into the town's best hotel and taking a bath, he still felt dusty and dirty. He also realized that his city clothes were totally unsuited for the dirty streets that became a sea of mud when it rained. When he felt comfortable with his new boots, wide brimmed cowboy hat, western shirt and trousers, he called on Mr. Fred Colbert, per instructions from Mr. Batchelder. Colonel Colbert as he preferred to be called, lived on a ranch several miles outside of town. His office contained a huge oaken desk with matching green-shaded lamps, surrounded by hunting trophies on the four walls. Crossed pistols and a Confederate flag completed the decor. After preliminary pleasantries, the Colonel applauded BM&G's idea of establishing retail operations in the West to sell Yankee hard goods and clothing. In spite of his comments, he really believed that eventually, the South would rise again and regain its economic importance. Peter withheld his thoughts, preferring to learn as much as he could from the old military man.

When Peter asked the Colonel where the best opportunity was, Colonel Colbert, without hesitation, slammed the desk with his hand and exclaimed, "Mexico, boy, Mexico, by gosh! Mexico is loaded with silver and has some gold to boot. Their operating mines have high grade ore but are under developed. The British know this and are starting to get very interested in investing, particularly where it's politically stable and where the government has their army troops in place. Mexico is still upset over losing the war with us and that damn Gadsden Treaty, but they'll get over it. I can get you connected with some of the wealthy families involved in silver mining and you'll be pleased with the results for sure. Whenever you're ready to go down to the Fresnillo area, just let me know, and I'll get you started with the right people. Don't worry about security, I'd send a couple of armed people I can trust down with you; you'd be safe."

Peter listened carefully to what the Colonel offered, but didn't like any part of going into a place where the military didn't like Americans. He'd also heard too many stories about visitors disappearing suddenly. No, he wasn't about to take on a risk of that magnitude. When Peter said that he had decided to not go into Mexico, Colonel Colbert replied, "Well, son, you can move on to the New Mexico Territory, but I wouldn't expect too much. And I'll tell you somethin' else; those Apache's ain't going to be waving any welcome flag out to you. There's more silver mining going on in Mexico than any place in the world, but if you've made up your mind, so be it."

Peter knew the Colonel was upset with him, but that still didn't change his mind. With a tip of his hat and a "thank you for everything, sir," he left the ranch and went back into town to get ready for the next stage for Tucson. The following morning, he checked the stage schedule and gathered his belongings, noting that the next trip would be leaving in two hours. After a brief lunch, he returned to the stage depot where he noted a very pretty young lady sitting on a bench with a pair of suitcases. As he sat down next to her, he doffed his hat and said, "Hi, I'm Peter Hillenbrand from New York, about to take the stage to Tucson. I hope you don't mind my sitting next to you; I thought perhaps I might be of service." Taken aback, the lady replied, "I'm also taking the stage, but only going as far as Ribera. My name is Kate Hurley, and I'm going to visit a relative in the town, which is about a day and a half's ride from here, I'm told. Please feel free to sit down, there aren't very many places left to rest."

Peter didn't know Ribera from Timbuktu, but became interested in getting to know this young lady a lot better. Maybe Ribera was worth taking a look at; there must be something going on in the place. They chatted briefly until the station master cried out, "All aboard for Tucson, Yuma, and San Diego and points between, all aboard! Be sure you take everything with you."

KONRAD BRUNER

Freiburg is home to Germany's world-renowned Institute of Mining and Metallurgy. Graduation day in June, 1858, was a special day for the parents and friends of Konrad Bruner, who was receiving his certificate with honors in Mining Technology. As proud and happy as his parents were on this day, Konrad was facing an uncertain future as he simply didn't know what he was going to do next. Without the prospect of a job, more schooling seemed to offer the best solution for the newly graduated engineer.

A year later, after completing studies at Heidelberg University, the economic climate had improved and he received a job offer that placed him in the iron and steel industry. The company, Alfred Krupp, located in Essen, was Germany's largest producer of iron, steel and heavy armaments. At Krupp, he became a novice engineer working in the open pit iron ore mines and iron casting foundries. He soon realized that the work was routine, boring and without challenge. More frustrating, his bosses didn't appreciate his suggestions for improvement even though they made sense and sometimes were eventually implemented. At one point, Hans von Brader, senior mining technician, bluntly told him to "stop offering your ideas; keep them to yourself, we have plenty of experts around here. Just do what we hired you to do." It also became apparent to Konrad that choice assignments were going to lesser qualified family relatives. After much soul searching, Konrad decided to leave Krupp and go into mining, the field he was most interested in. His parents were horrified that he would resign from such a prestigious company, but Konrad knew he was faced with a dead end and stuck to his decision.

When Bruner submitted his resignation, von Brader was upset that he would "do such a thing, particularly after all I've done for you." In reality, Konrad was departing over what the boss hadn't done for him, but he only smiled, swallowed his pride, and moved on.

The young German bid goodbye to his family and left continental Europe, crossing the English channel, entraining for the Cornwall tin-mining district. In the late-1850's, the Cornwall area was well developed, thanks to the invention of huge, dewatering, steam driven pumps that enabled the mine owners to dig far deeper than anyone else in the world. These machines and the Cornish miners kept the British in the forefront of deep mining technology, especially where flooding was a major problem. Within a week, Konrad Bruner was working for Cornwall Tin Limited, starting underground under the tutelage of an experienced mine foreman. When not in the mine, he studied and learned to speak, read and write English. Always with a slight Teutonic accent, however.

At Cornwall Tin Limited, his diligence and training soon qualified him for more responsibility and he was promoted to a foreman position, much to the chagrin of his English associates. Management soon recognized that he was their most capable engineer in drilling, blasting and mucking techniques. He also offered new concepts on timbering which increased productivity. These accomplishments only angered his peers further to the point that he was shunned by most of them socially.

When there was a serious accident in Section B of the mine, the English engineers placed the blame collectively on the "arrogant German and his newfangled ideas." The death of several miners gave the press the ammunition to criticize and headline the passive owners, who deplored the adverse publicity. Faced with pressure from the miners, engineering staff and the press, the board of directors searched for a scapegoat and found one in Konrad Bruner. When the London board passed the word to terminate the services of Bruner, no one in operations came to his defense and he was fired.

Realizing that no company in England would hire him, Konrad went back to his flat, not knowing what he would do next. An envelope was tacked to his door that contained a message from Sir Clarence Bingham, president of Cornwall Tin Limited. The note invited him to visit the executive on the following Thursday, at his private home. Stunned, Bruner couldn't contemplate what the old gentleman had in mind, but certainly, best he find out.

In his study, Sir Clarence began: "Mr. Bruner, I know the past week or so has been a terrible experience for you. I want you to know that I do not hold you responsible for the deaths of the three miners. I consider you to be one of the best engineers that has ever worked for our company. Initially, I thought I might have you transferred to another mine we own, but the directors would have none of it. Most of my associates in London have never been underground in one of our mines, so have little appreciation for the hazardous work we do every single day. Unfortunately, they are also scared to death of adverse publicity and criticism from the government and press. Their decision is final, but in recognition of your work with us, I want to help you get reestablished. Please, consider this. I have a very good friend in Mexico who owns several large silver properties in the Zacatecas area. I know the family well, having worked there for several years as a mining consultant. Amelio Rodriguez is a wealthy man who I hold in the highest regard. He has been writing to me for the past year, seeking my advice on a host of problems he has with his mines and smelters. Their technology and production methods are way behind Cornwall standards. I believe you could be a big help to Amelio in modernizing his operations. There's no doubt in my mind that, with my recommendation, he would be happy to employ your services. That is contained in the enclosed letter of introduction, which I'd like you to read."

Scanning the letter, Konrad was embarrassed, but felt vindicated after what his peers had put him through. "I'm also providing you with a small severance allowance of fifty pounds in recognition of the good work you've done here that should cover your expenses to Mexico, if you decide to go. If you decide not to go, please keep the money to help you get started somewhere else; you've earned it."

Surprised but flattered, Konrad muttered a brief thank-you as he left Sir Clarence's estate. Later, collecting his thoughts of that afternoon's experience, Bruner realized that he was vindicated over his commitment to safety as a key method of improving productivity. He also gave some serious thoughts on how he might improve his own social skills, working with miners, peers and management.

The four-week trip from Plymouth to Tampico was a tonic for Konrad Bruner. He had a comfortable stateroom, he had freedom to roam the ship and the food and company was reasonable. He was also able to study several of the recently published books on mining technology bought in Truro, before he embarked to leave England. On arrival in Mexico, he arranged to ride to the silver mining district, where Senor Rodriguez made his home.

When Amelio Rodriguez read the introductory letter given to him by Bruner, the Mexican was ecstatic. "Senor Bruner, you will stay at my hacienda and enjoy the hospitality of my family until we decide on where you will fit into our plans and where you would like to live. This letter from Sir Clarence, an old and very dear friend, is beyond my best expectations for our mines, but also to meet a new friend. Welcome, from the bottom of my heart."

Before discussing business, the patron escorted the engineer around his estate on two magnificent steeds. The properties contained not only mines and smelters, but huge expanses of crops growing, vineyards and thousands of grazing cattle. The expanse of land ownership was more than the German could comprehend. Beyond the Zacatecas operations, Rodriguez also had docks and warehouses in Tampico and Vera Cruz, fishing fleets in the Sea of Cortez and factories in Mexico City producing clothing, mining tools, building materials and furniture. He also traded in precious metals for export.

His indoctrination to the Rodriguez family was crowned by his introduction to Luisa Rodriguez, the only daughter of Amelio, at a patio luncheon several weeks after his arrival in Mexico. She was nineteen, with olive complexion, long black hair, dark eyes, and a smile that would melt anything human. "Mein Gott," breathed Konrad, "this is the most beautiful woman I have ever seen in my life." Very few words were spoken however, as Anna Maria, her chaperone, cast beady eyes at the German. It was revealed that Luisa had been away in Mexico City, studying Latin and French, and being introduced to Mexican high society. Her poise and friendliness left Konrad speechless. It also extended his residency at the hacienda.

Every once in a while, Konrad joined Amelio and Luisa on horseback rides to visit the herds or supervise the selection of a prize bull for breeding. On these outings, Anna Maria stayed at the hacienda which allowed Konrad and Luisa to speak to one another as normal young people do. Konrad fell in love with the young beauty, believing that Luisa was more than casually interested in him, and he was right. In spite of the overbearance of Anna Maria, a timely smile, a brief secret touch cemented the lovers' desire to explore their relationship further.

Deeper involvement was short-circuited by the patron's suggestion that it was time to visit the mines where production was lagging significantly. He introduced Konrad to his superintendent, Carlos Ortega, who would conduct the tour.

Over the course of the next two weeks, the two descended to working levels, viewed crushing equipment, hoisting practices and overall labor management. Carlos was well acquainted with the problems, calling attention to inadequate training and lack of investment in machinery as major causes of declining production. Bruner was basically in agreement with the Mexican's assessment. Carlos had also done an excellent job of collecting and filing exploratory drill hole data and logging core specimens. On his return to the hacienda, he met with Amelio to review the results of his examination. "Senor, you have a substantial position in this silver mining district. While production has slacked off some, most of it is due to mining lower grade ores and not reduced productivity from the workers. You have a very capable superintendent in Carlos Ortega, who knows your operations well and is respected by everyone. We believe that you can make substantial cost reductions by investing in an upgraded hoisting system and installing additional ventilation equipment. We have estimated your proven reserves to be at least twice what you have on your records which means you will be able to mine economically for at least another fifty years. I would suggest you appoint Carlos to head up these improvements, which should begin immediately. Once these improvements are underway, I will begin to study your metallurgical processes and look for ways to improve recoveries of silver and lead as a secondary product."

Amelio Rodriguez was overwhelmed with the report. It meant solid future earnings for his holdings and the ability to invest in other industries that were beginning to show promise. "This young man has the capability to manage all my mining operations and to do it well. He's honest, seems to be attracted to Luisa … I wonder, what can I do to keep him here?"

Once new equipment was installed, operations showed gradual but continuous improvement, as Konrad had expected. He turned his interest to training a couple of young geologists to map new portions of the underground workings and began work on the milling and smelting practices.

Unfortunately, his desire to build a close relationship with Luisa was not going as well. The intrusiveness of Anna Maria was only a small part of the problem. As their love for one another had blossomed, respect for their individual religious beliefs had solidified into an impasse. Under the surveillance of the chaperone, they talked endlessly about the Lutheran and Catholic churches, always failing to reach any serious compromise.

Perhaps it was the silver mine successes, maybe the impossible love affair with Luisa or just plain wanderlust that led Konrad to consider moving on. He knew that he could marry and live prosperously in Mexico, but somehow the appeal was no longer foremost in his mind. Conversion to Luisa's church was not something he was prepared to do and the problem became insurmountable. The desire someday to be his own boss was another serious part of his personal struggle.

When he decided to leave Mexico he tried to explain his decision to Luisa, who was devastated. "I was afraid this might happen, Konrad, but hoped and prayed that we could somehow reach a compromise. You have lived here with my family long enough to realize that my faith in the Catholic Church is the foundation of my life and everything I want to do in my lifetime. This is a sorry ending for both of us; I will always love you." The heartbreaking conversation was followed by a brief embrace, quietly witnessed by the unsmiling Anna Maria.

Konrad made his usual rounds to explain his plans to leave Mexico. Everyone wished him well, for they had grown to admire the German engineer. When he finally returned to the great house, he climbed the stairs and went to his room. It was in the heat of the day and the household was in siesta. As he readied himself for a nap, he heard a gentle tapping on his heavy, oaken entryway. Opening the door, he saw Luisa, who had her forefinger over her mouth, suggesting silence.

She quickly crossed the threshold, closed the door, putting her arms around Bruner's neck and passionately kissed him. He hardened spontaneously, lost in the sensuous embrace. "Konrad, oh Konrad," she whispered as she loosened her blouse, moving toward the bed. As she let her crenulated skirt drop to the floor, she pulled the covers back, saying, "My darling, it's all right. I cannot contain my love for you any longer. I want you, please." In a passionate frenzy, Bruner removed his clothes and joined her in their first sexual encounter, which was explosive and passionate.

Lying in Konrad's arms, Luisa confessed, "I am so sorry to put you through this, but I could not contain my love for you any longer. I put some ground cocoa leaves in Anna Maria's wine at lunch, so we could have a few hours together. She'll be asleep for most of the afternoon. Mother and father are out inspecting cattle and won't be home until later this evening. Please forgive me for acting like a woman of the streets, but I wanted to show you my love before you left us." Dazed, but happy and excited with the prospect of further lovemaking, Konrad murmured, "Luisa, you have captured my heart; I will always love you." Embracing each other tightly, the couple again relieved their passion with furious lovemaking. "Dear Konrad, do not despair. What we have done will be forgiven by God. I must leave you now, but let's go for a late afternoon ride when Anna Marie awakens. That way, she will never suspect what we will treasure for the rest of our lives."

On the final evening with the family, Senor Rodriguez rose to give a toast. "Konrad Bruner, we don't want you to leave us and Mexico. I had visions of you being a member of this family, and I'm heavy in my heart that it couldn't be worked out. You have honored my household for over three years and we will always remember you. However, I must respect your wishes. The journey to El Paso is not to be trifled with. It will be long and difficult because the trail is rugged and infested with banditos, renegade Confederate army veterans and of course our own corrupt police. Americans underestimate the terrorizing by the Apache Indians and what they have done in the New Mexico Territory and in

Sonora and Chihuahua. So, I hope you will allow me to have Lumberto accompany you on your journey north. You may see him as my trusted, unassuming valet, but believe me, he is a warrior with much experience dealing with the hazards of travel in our country. He is an expert pistol and rifle shot, but most important, will be your loyal campadre on this dangerous trip. He will keep you safe and stay with you as long as you need him. This is a very sad day for me, amigo. Remember, this will always be your home." Lifting a glass of red wine, he said, "Now my friend, vaya con dios." Holding back tears, Luisa smiled at Konrad and lifted her glass in salute. She also secretly prayed that Konrad's seed would grow within her and produce a love child.

Six weeks after leaving the Rodriguez hacienda, Lumberto and Konrad splashed across the shallow, muddy waters of the Rio Grande River and entered Texas. The trip had been fearful at times; only the quick thinking of Lumberto, and a few gold coins, had gotten them through several encounters with banditos and Federale police. Tired, grimy and hungry, the two horsemen reined in at the Coronado Hotel in El Paso. The horses were led to the livery stable, then the two riders went to their rooms for a thorough bath, and then, some food.

DALE NEWPORT

The River Bend Ranch was the largest spread in the Bowie River Valley. It covered over 100,000 acres outside of town and was owned by Dale Newport and his family. Approximately 3,000 head of cattle roamed the meadows and foothills, getting fat on some of the finest grass in the territory. In the northwest portion of the ranch, the senior Newport bred and tended to over 1,000 horses that he periodically sold to the U.S. Army. About 50 acres of the ranch were devoted to irrigated grain and vegetable farming, managed by Garland Newport, her daughter Dolores and son-in-law Don Richmond. At lower elevations, juniper and scrub oak dominated the landscape; over 6,000 feet, the hills were covered with lodgepole and ponderosa pine.

The most important feature of the terrain was the southern boundary of the property, which abutted the Bowie River, which flowed year round. Rising over a hundred miles away in the mountains of the New Mexico Territory, the Bowie was the life blood of the River Bend Ranch and the Ribera community. Until the post-Civil War period, usage of the river water was never an issue as there was always sufficient flow to satisfy the needs of the ranch and citizenry. The discovery of gold in the river and the influx of settlers looking for good land and water were about to change this placid scene forever.

Dale Newport was born in Washington County, Ohio, assuming ownership of the family farm when his parents died. He raised corn and grains to support a few cattle and pigs, which were bartered with other farmers in the area for required living necessities. Periodically, the Ohio River, clogged with spring ice, thawed and flooded its banks, wiping away plantings, homes, barns and equipment. This natural disaster, twice in four years, convinced Dale that it was time to move on to higher ground, which he located in Missouri. Two years of inadequate rainfall and tornadoes forced him and the family to again relocate, this time to Ribera, New Mexico Territory. Hardened by previous failures, Dale Newport set out to build the largest cattle herd in the valley. This time, no excuses; he was going to succeed.

His first, modest purchase was from the estate of Roger Kiley, who had died while the property was in default. Under intense pressure from the local bank, the widow Kiley caved in and Dale Newport paid her an undervalued amount to secure the land.

Dale built his herd rapidly by scouring the countryside for unbranded strays. While it was common practice at the time, Dale Newport was far more aggressive than other ranchers and cleverly grew and prospered. When challenged by neighbors, he continued to expand by either buying them out or forcing them into receivership. His ally in these transactions was Brad Scoville, the local banker, who conspired with Dale on most of these deals. In the process, both men became feared, but not respected, in the community. Neither man cared what the townspeople thought of them or their business transactions. Nor did they trust one another, recognizing that the accumulation of individual wealth was what counted most.

Dale Newport was married to Garland Newport and had two grown children. Dolores, the oldest, was an attractive woman with auburn hair and an engaging smile. She got along well with the townspeople and was a close friend of Barbara Casey, who owned the local general store. Dolores was married to Don Richmond, a graduate veterinarian, who specialized in large animals. He spent most of his time doctoring River Bend Ranch animals and improving the herds by careful selection of the best stallions and bulls. He rarely got involved with other ranchers in the community and stayed clear of his father-in-law as much as possible. At times, he felt that he and Dolores should leave Ribera, but Dolores was too close to her Mom to consider such a move. She also loved the ranch, was very knowledgeable of the animals, crops grown and importance of the river water to the success of their operation. Her fondest hope was that Dad would leave the ranch to her and her brother when he passed on, or at least a portion of it, where she and Don could be on their own.

Greg Newport, at twenty years of age, was built like his father; short, stocky and rough-hewn. He functioned as the ranch's general foreman, but actually ran things more and more as his father's health declined. It made Garland very uncomfortable because Greg was aggressive and short-tempered. She worried further because he was very excitable and inclined to act before thinking. He was disliked by most of the locals as he tended to act superior and throw his weight around. He spent most Saturday nights drinking with his ranch hands at the saloons in town, followed by an excursion to Corrinne's place, Ribera's house of ill repute. As embarrassing as his nocturnal activities were to the family, Dale refused to intervene, in spite of his wife's insistence that he "should do something to curb this boy's immoral behavior." He would only say, "He's a young man just blowing off a little steam; he'll grow out of it shortly, believe me." In his heart, though, he was very disturbed about his son's behavior, combative nature and recklessness.

Dale Newport had to be pleased with the agreement reached with General Bradley at Fort Bliss, where he had negotiated two contracts to supply beef cattle and horses to army installations in Arizona and New Mexico. They were ambitious obligations, but with a little bit of luck from the weather, he was confident he would be able to meet the delivery dates. As he rode the stage from Fort Bliss to El Paso, he began to think of the River Bend Ranch and some of its problems.

The ranch itself was in excellent shape. The herds of cattle and horses were healthy and growing; the farming operation was contributing well to the business. Only last week, Dolores had signed a contract with Pryor's livery stable to supply wheat, barley and oats on a regular basis. Even the garden patch was producing far more corn, beans, peas, cauliflower and broccoli than the ranch could consume.

What concerned him most was how the next generation would handle things after he died. His recent visit with the doctor had been very discouraging and probably a wake-up call that he would prefer to ignore, but couldn't, any longer. Doc Gilroy had been unusually persistent in telling Dale that his heart was deteriorating and that he had to slow down, or risk a stroke or heart attack. He made it clear that his irregular heart beat and chest pains were a serious warning. Dale had tried to slow down, but still insisted on joining Greg and the boys at roundup. He knew Garland was worried about his health and no longer content to hear him respond with, "Don't you worry about ole Dale, honey, I'm getting along just fine." He also knew that Garland saw through his remarks like a pane of glass. He just didn't want to talk about retirement and deciding who was going to take over the ranch when he died.

Dale Newport really did believe Doc Gilroy's medical analysis. At the same time, he wasn't prepared to formally announced that Greg was the new, sole owner of the River Bend Ranch. He loved his son, but was certain that he was far too immature to take the reins at this time. Without changing a few habits, maybe never. He was bright enough, but didn't have the experience or temperament to deal with the likes of Scoville, Sheriff Bellows and Barbara Casey, probably the smartest one of the bunch. Had he failed somewhere along the line to train Greg and prepare him for managing things?

The more he thought about the problem, the more he realized that Dolores was more qualified to run the ranch. Though Dale didn't particularly cotton to her husband, he trusted the man and suspected the two of them would run things capably. Dolores was like her mother; pretty, intelligent and with good common sense.

He'd never discussed the problem with Garland because he knew she'd give him the answer he didn't want to hear. "But, goldarnit, how could I possibly turn the ranch over to a woman, no matter how capable she is?" As in previous similar dilemmas, he decided to do nothing. "What the hell, if I die in the saddle, they'll figure something out. Maybe I should just stop frettin', and let nature take its course."

Once he decided to postpone the ownership issue, he began to concentrate on how to deal with the newcomers on the Bowie River. Since the gold strike, all sorts of prospectors, miners, and attendant hustlers had moved into the area to create a new, unregulated mass of humanity that were focused on gold, and only gold. The town of Ribera was prospering with the discovery, but his ranch and water rights were being abused. The sheriff was ignoring the problem, not making any move to protect Newport's property. And Garland had complained that the irrigation water for the vegetable farm was heavily silted. The more he thought about the problem, the more he realized it was up to him to take control. The river was full of diggers, the water was becoming polluted and gravel was being piled up, diverting normal flows. And, he wasn't sharing in the new wealth for the community. "They're tearing up my land, depositing their gold into Scoville's bank and spending the extra at the general store or in the beer halls and hotel."

He wasn't very happy with Brad Scoville's reaction when he mentioned the problem to him. When he'd complained, Brad had come back with, "Relax, Dale, you're fussin' over something that isn't that serious. They ain't causing all that much trouble and the gold they're pulling out of the river is sure as hell good for the town. Just ask Barbara at the general store, Clyde Bond at the assay office or the guys at the hotel and saloons. They raise a little hell on Saturday night, but otherwise, aren't much of a bother. When was the last time the sheriff had to clap one of those boys into jail. Come on, Dale, you're getting worked up over nothing but a fly speck."

Newport was surprised at Scoville's remarks, but said nothing. As he left the banker's office, he wondered how Brad had suddenly become so friendly with miners. The more he thought about it, the more he realized that the miners were depositing more gold into the Mercantile Bank than Brad had ever seen before. Why wouldn't he like it? "Good God, I've been half asleep these past few months. Brad and the town don't have any interest in curbing the miners; the money is rolling in, and Tent City is far enough away that they don't see or hear anything!"

The more Dale Newport thought about the situation and the sheriff's inaction, the more his temperature rose. "Well, folks, you've ignored me long enough. Sheriff Bellows gets cracking to stop these river rats and if nothing happens, I'm going to do what I know has to be done. I'll get Greg to hire us a few hard cases from out of town so we can get started. A couple of extra guns will tell people that we're through getting pushed around by the miners. Most of these people don't remember what this town was like in the old days. They don't know how mean a cuss I can be." Once he'd made up his mind, Dale relaxed and drifted off to sleep to the swaying motion of the stagecoach.

EL PASO TO RIBERA

The stage ride from the West Texas border to Ribera was a 250-mile stretch through high, rugged mountains, desert plains and intermittent river crossings. Apache Indians, renegade Confederate sympathizers and bands of Mexican bandits roamed the area. U.S. Army troops, recalled East during the Civil War, were only beginning to reclaim control of the area.

Among the worst were former Confederates who viewed General Lee as a traitor for surrendering at Appomattox. Some were genuine military committed to resuming the struggle, many were just plain thugs with an excuse to rob and kill to line their pockets. While army forts were being re-established on the frontier, the Indians and crooks enjoyed "open season" on the few settlers and people crossing the territory. Still, pioneers like John Butterfield fought hard to establish safe transportation between San Antonio and San Diego. Skeptics of this start-up enterprise ridiculed the Overland Mail as "running from nowhere through nothing, to no place."

To provide some security for the trace, the company established small stockades where horses could be exchanged and passengers get a hot meal and a brief rest. Salty Fleming and his shotgun companion were experienced drivers, but on this trip they were delayed getting through the desert because of severe dust storms and problems at two of the major river crossings.

When they pulled into Pontello Springs, the passengers were cranky and exhausted. As they stepped down from the stagecoach, Peter Hillenbrand berated the drivers with insulting remarks. He was complaining bitterly until Dale Newport pulled him aside, saying, "Son, you're gonna have big problems out here if you treat people this way. These guys are only doing their best under very nasty conditions. Wind, dust storms and flash floods go with the territory here and you'd best get accustomed to delays and inconveniences. I'd suggest you apologize to the drivers and keep your advice to yourself." Shocked by Newport's put-down, but repentant, "PH" sought out Salty, apologized and meekly entered the adobe building, which served as the kitchen and dining room. His fellow passengers, including Kate Hurley, said little over the altercation.

In spite of the late hour, Pablo and Maria Sanchez were well prepared for the troop with fried bacon, corn bread, pinto beans and coffee. As they devoured the hot food, Salty explained that the delay meant a very short night if they were going to arrive in Ribera at least close to their original schedule. With groans of acceptance, the travel party murmured a collective "good night" and fell off to sleep.

Shortly before dawn, two men, dressed as Apache Indians, silently subdued the night guard at the corral, gagged him and tied him to a post behind the stage house. They also warned him, "Now you keep quiet. Make any kind of a noise and you're a dead man." One of the "Indians" mouthed a coyote call, signaling to their partners that it was all clear to take the station. Moving swiftly, the gang burst into the building with guns drawn, shouting, "Get on the floor and keep your hands on your heads if you want to live." Salty shouted, "Do as they say," realizing that they had little choice but to hope that it was only a robbery taking place. His main obligation was to see that the passengers didn't resist and end up getting killed.

The gang then proceeded to search each passenger, relieving them of money watches, guns and other valuables. Dale Newport had a derringer hidden in his vest, but was in no position to use it, at least at this time. Konrad Bruner's equipment bag was examined but left intact. Doctor Ben Lawson's medical kit also passed inspection, including a bank draft for $4,500, which had been wrapped in bandages. They also missed $500 in cash, tightly secured in the lining of his coat. The gang leader then ordered Salty Fleming to get the strong box from the stagecoach, and promptly shot the lock off. They were unhappy, with less than $2,500 in cash and gold contained in the box.

As the sun rose, one gang member stared intently at Bart LaGrange, who was trying to be as inconspicious as possible. Gus Tomber told Bart to stand up and remove his hat. When LaGrange did what he was told, Tomber lunged forward, cracking Bart across the head with his pistol, dropping the escaped convict to the floor. As the passengers looked on in sheer terror, Gus Tomber seethed, "Sum' bitch, I knowed I'd seen him before. Let's bring him along to camp with us and

I'll tell you guys a lot more about him. I sure as hell want to ask him a few questions." Unconscious and bleeding from the head wound, LaGrange was lifted into an empty saddle and his hands tied to the horn to keep him upright with the help of one of the gang riders.

As the bandits disappeared eastward, Salty Fleming gathered the rattled group in the stage station to talk to them. He told them, "We got a big break last night; nobody was killed. I'm sorry the lady lost her jewelry, maybe next time you'll keep it hidden like you were told to by the company. By now you've probably figured out they weren't Apache Injuns, even with the buckskin clothing and war paint on 'em. I don't know why they went to all that trouble, unless they're trying to keep the army troops confused and chasin' real Indians. Why they took Mr. LaGrange hostage is spooky to me. There's lots of discharged Rebel soldiers out this way; maybe they were buddies or enemies at one time. I'm gonna check the "Wanted" posters in town when we get there, to see if I can recognize any of 'em. Sorry for all the excitement; let's grab a quick biscuit and coffee and get outa here as soon as we can."

As the stage rumbled through the mountains, Dale Newport, sometimes dozing off, found himself profiling each one of the passengers. "That banker youngster from New York is a real greenhorn, but handled himself pretty well with the robbers. I didn't see him sweatin' too hard; maybe he'll be all right out here. A few of the boys at the bunkhouse could sure give him an instruction or two. He'll either learn fast or be on his way in a month or two. The German guy? Says he's worked in Old Mexico in the silver mines. Speaks darn good English. Maybe he's heard about the gold strike on the Bowie River. He could be an interesting addition to the community; I just hope he doesn't side in with those diggers. Lawson seems young for a graduated M.D. but that's probably just me. I didn't catch why he's going to Ribera, but I'll bet Doc Gilroy would be happy to have him stay a while. I'll let him figure out what's going on. Now that Kate Hurley sure is a looker. She talked a lot with Hillenbrand, but hell, that's only natural. I wonder how much of that city bullshit she believed. God, if only Greg could hook up with someone like her, settle down and raise a family; life would sure get simpler."

As the stage coach horses galloped through the countryside, the orange-red sunset turned into darkness. It was ominously quiet except for the occasional cry of an animal or the yelling of the driver. As they crossed the Bowie River ten miles north of town, the lights of Ribera glowed in the darkness. An hour later, Salty and his partner brought the Concord to an abrupt, skidding halt before the

Whitman Hotel and its attached saloon. Its doors flew open as the bartender shouted, above the din, "Boys, the stage is finally in."

Goodbyes were brief; most of the passengers were tired and just wanted to get out of the coach, stretch their legs and breathe some fresh air. Bruner, Hillenbrand and Dr. Ben Lawson retrieved their luggage from the stage and trudged to the hotel lobby to register. Dale Newport was met by his son Greg, who weaved out of the saloon towards a wagon and team at the livery stable. Kate Hurley, the only female passenger arrival, was duly noted by the locals. One bright young cowboy summed it up by saying, "Hey, things may be looking up in this here town after all."

Barbara Casey had been worried sick over the stage coach's delay. When she stepped toward her niece, both burst into tears and hugged one another, saying nothing. Finally, Barbara said, "Kate, I'm so glad to see you, I don't know what to say. Let's get back to the house before I make a bigger fool of myself. Just tell Enrique here what bags are yours and we'll be on our way; it's just around the corner." Enrique smiled at the prospect of a visitor to Barbara Casey; perhaps the girl would not only help in the store, but also bring some sunshine into her Aunt Barbara's life.

THE OCOTILLO MINE

Dr. Ben Lawson rubbed his eyes and opened them, wondering where he was. He scratched his head and stretched his arms and legs in an attempt to shake off his weariness. Sunshine brightened the room; gradually he remembered checking in to the Whitman Hotel the previous evening and collapsing into bed. Surveying the room, he noted that his baggage and medical kit were where he'd dropped them when he got to his room last night. He lurched to the window, listening to the sounds of riders on horseback, creaking wagons and human voices. In the distance, a dog barked. Sticking his head out the window, he looked over the main street of the town of Ribera. Scanning the buildings, he could see a bank, general store, assay office, and saloon. At the far end of town, he could make out the livery stable and corrals. He became fully awake when he spotted a weathered sign with a painted "Henry J. Gilroy, Medical Doctor" over a small office. He decided to visit the doctor after getting some food in his belly and depositing his Dad's money in the local bank.

He splashed cold water on his face, shaved and went to the hotel dining room, where he saw Peter Hillenbrand talking with a waitress as he finished his coffee. Ben nodded briefly, opting to read the local paper instead of chatting with the young banker. He'd heard enough stories about New York and the hustle bustle of the big city. He ordered a steak with beans and settled down to read about the influx of prospectors and miners, and the explosive growth of Tent City. Most of the remaining news was pretty routine, sprinkled with local advertisements for the livery stable, assay office and various stores. Nothing about the stage coach robbery, but it was too early to expect any news there. Finishing breakfast and a second cup of coffee, he was ready to walk around town and get acquainted. He left the hotel and crossed the wide, heavily rutted Main Street.

The bank teller, noting the size of Ben's deposit, ushered the doctor into Brad Scoville's office for a formal introduction. Scoville offered Lawson an overstuffed chair facing his desk and provided Ben with a brief history of the town, and its rapid growth, accelerated by a recent placer gold strike. Coupled with ranching and a stage line connecting Tucson with El Paso, the banker felt that more growth and more people could be expected. He was certain that Doc Gilroy, the town's only doctor, would be happy to see another physician come to town. The deposit recorded, Ben thanked Scoville for his hospitality and left, to continue his exploration of the town.

Ben walked down the main street to introduce himself to Doc Gilroy. His door was unlocked but it appeared that the man was probably out on a call. Ben left a message saying he'd be back in an hour or so. A couple of store fronts ahead, Ben entered the assay office run by Clyde Bond. Bond was a tall, thin man who greeted him with a warm hello as he entered the store, which was stocked with picks, shovels, and several sizes of panning dishes. When Clyde learned that Ben was related to Tom Lawson, he brightened considerably. "Sure, I know Tom, but haven't seen him in months; but I know he's still up near Growler Creek doing something. He's very secretive about his claim; I haven't done any assay work for him, but that's probably because I won't give him any more credit until he pays me what he already owes me. Here, let me show you what he bought from me." Clyde then showed Ben a list of hand tools bought several months ago that amounted to over two hundred dollars. "I'm pretty sure he's all right, 'cause diggers see him from time to time as they move up the river. I'd sure be much obliged if you would take care of what he owes me."

Ben wasn't quite ready to open his wallet on such short notice, telling Clyde, "Once I find Tom, I'm sure we will take care of whatever is owed you. In the meantime, maybe you can give me directions to where Tom is working."

Strolling back on the boardwalk to the hotel, Ben noticed that Doc Gilroy's door was open. He crossed over, walked into the office and introduced himself. The Doc, a short, overweight man, got up from behind a table, covered with medical books, bottles of pills, and bandages. His smile was friendly and genuine; Ben liked him immediately.

"Well, Dr. Lawson, I'm sure glad to see ya'; sit down and tell me all about yourself. Where are you from; did you go to a real medical school; what brings you to Ribera? Are you gonna stay here or are you just passing through?" Ben gave Doc answers to most of his questions, but didn't say much about how long he'd be staying in the town. He also stated that he didn't come to Ribera to compete with Dr. Gilroy; he was here to look up his brother Tom and help him with a few things.

Doc Gilroy responded with a laugh, saying, "If you went to a real medical school, I don't think you'd want to start your practice in a place like this. I handle miner accidents, gunshot wounds, a few cracked skulls once in a while and birthing babies. A lot of times, people don't have money to pay me; I end up with all kinds of stuff, like bales of hay, jars of food, animals; you name it. I manage to barter what I receive for my needs with the folks in town. I get by, but I'll never be rich, I'll tell you. Trust me, there's not much here, excepting the miners, and most of them would rather throw their money away on liquor and loose women than pay me. If you ever get called to go to Tent City, get paid in advance. It's not a pretty picture down there.

"On the other hand, I'd jump up and down if you were to locate here; there's enough medical work here for three doctors. I expect with your formal training, I'd be able to learn a thing or two. Most learnin' I got came by way of books published way before the Civil War. So, I welcome you and hope you'll stay here awhile."

Doc Gilroy didn't know Tom Lawson directly, but had seen him in town and knew him by reputation. He figured Tom had been in the area about a year, working as a loner. He'd panned for a while where Tent City is today, but didn't stay long when it started to get crowded. He moved upriver to where Growler Creek comes in and as far as he knew, that was where he was now. "You're probably anxious to locate Tom, but when you get back in town, come on over to the house and I'll have Mrs. Cawley fix us a real, home-cooked dinner. Remember, he's about twenty miles up the Bowie where Growler Creek comes in. I don't think you'll have any trouble finding the place. Be sure you're armed, there's no telling when a stray Apache gets down that way."

After talking to Barney Pryor at the livery stable, Ben walked up the street and entered Barbara Casey's general store. He was surprised to see Kate Hurley talking to a customer; she looked real pretty in a long dress with a red ribbon in her hair. As Barbara Casey approached, he again glanced at Kate and decided he liked what he saw a lot. Mrs. Casey caught his glance, but only smiled and offered to help him pick out riding boots and clothing. Making polite conversation, she asked him how long he was going to be in town. "Mrs. Casey, I'm here to meet up with my brother Tom, who is prospecting in the area. I haven't seen him in over four years." Barbara Casey hadn't made the connection between the two, but quickly recovered. With Tom owing her a lot of money, she decided to open the subject with Ben.

"Dr. Lawson, I have a serious problem with your brother. He came in here several months ago and I allowed him to buy clothes, blankets, cooking equipment and a tent, promising to pay me within a month. It's been over three months and I haven't heard a word from Tom. I trusted the man and he's taken advantage of me. I hope that when you find him, you can help me get my money; it's over four hundred dollars. I can't run my business this way." Ben explained that he would be leaving tomorrow to visit Tom and promised that the bill would be taken care of when he returned, in a week or so. It wasn't the answer Barbara was looking for, but she recognized that she had very little choice, at least at this time. Tom's money problems upset Ben, but aside from the back bills, he seemed to be pretty well liked. Barbara Casey was more annoyed than the assayer, but then again, she was owed a lot more money. Kate Hurley waved to him with a big smile as he left the store.

Leaving the general store, he was met by Sam Bellows, sheriff of Ribera. They exchanged pleasantries, Sam asked how long he intended to stay in Ribera. "I'm not sure, Sheriff; it all depends on what I find out when I see my brother Tom. It could be a year or shorter. By the way, I'm going up that way tomorrow and would like to buy a pistol and rifle to keep me company. Just about everyone has warned me about Apaches in the area. I'm not a sharpshooter, but have used both in the past. I know which end of the gun the bullet comes out of." The sheriff smiled and told Ben, "I can loan you a pistol we took from a man a few months ago. It's a model 1848 pocket revolver called a baby dragoon, that's easy to carry. Hang onto it as long as you need it; the owner won't be looking for it. He's buried in Boot Hill just outside of town. If you're serious about a rifle, I'd check with Barney Pryor at the livery stable; he seems to have collected a few. I doubt that you'll need one, but suit yourself. C'mon down to the jail house, I'll get you that baby dragoon." The sheriff checked Ben out with the pistol, at the same time asking him questions about the hold-up at Pontello Springs. Ben added a few details of the kidnapping of Bart LaGrange, then left the jail to return to the hotel for a nap.

When he awoke, he bought dinner at the hotel, dining quietly by himself.

The next morning, Ben went to the livery stable and rented two horses; one for riding, the other for carrying provisions for a three-day trip up the Bowie River. He discussed the purchase of a single short Sharp's rifle, but decided to pass on the idea. Barney wasn't particularly interested in selling the rifle anyway and agreed with the sheriff that it probably wasn't necessary. "Hell I'd worry more about rattlesnakes and cougars than I would injuns."

Riding out of town, Lawson glanced to the northeast to snow-capped Mt. Cody, an extinct volcano that rose to 9,200 feet. It was an impressive sight, some twenty-five miles away. Staying close to the riverbed, he covered the distance to Growler Creek by late afternoon. As he reached a break in the ground cover, he spurred his horse up a slight hill towards the noise of several voices. Passing a heap of mine tailings, he came to a clearing where a group of Mexicans were eating. One stood up and shouted "Alto," covering Ben with a rifle. Startled, Ben raised his hands, asking for Senor Thomaso, who was his "hermano." One of the men entered the mine tunnel and within a few minutes a dusty, dirty Tom Lawson, almost unrecognizable, emerged from the portal. Quizzically, he looked at Ben, muttering, "Look, this here's private property; just what are you doing up here?" Beating dust from his shirt and trousers he gave the visitor a second look, finally exclaiming, "Oh my gosh, it's you, Ben! God, is it good to see you. I hadn't heard a word about my letter; I wasn't even sure you'd received it. I couldn't figure if Dad was going to come through with the money or disown me. By golly, it sure looks like you're growed some. Get down off that horse so I can give you the grand tour of my strike. Felipe, take care of my brother's horses, while I show him around."

For the next hour, the brothers talked about home, how Dad was getting along, how Ebbie was doing and Dad's decision to provide development money for the mine. Tom was overjoyed to realize he could continue working the mine and start moving some of the ore to the smelter to generate cash.

"Dad and Ebbie will be happy to hear that you're okay and getting along all right. I've deposited $5,000 in the Mercantile Bank under both our names. It sure helped to make a few friends pretty fast. So tell me, what can I do to help you?"

Tom answered, "I owe some money to a few of the people in town, which I'd like to get paid off; I need to get in touch with the smelter people in Copper Flats and figure how to get stockpiled ore to them. I'm thinking of buying a few wagons and mules to get started. If you could help me on those things, it would take a heckuva load off of my mind."

In the next couple of days, Tom's success story gradually came out. He'd been in Utah and New Mexico, before deciding to go to Ribera. He'd panned for gold near Tent City, but when the California miners converged on the area, he had decided to follow the river northeast. At first, he concentrated on gold panning and was modestly successful. Near Growler Creek, he discovered tiny veinlets in an outcrop of a gray mineral that he couldn't identify. He thought about taking samples to Clyde Bond for analysis, but knew he'd want some money up front first. He did stake his claim in Copper Flats and in talking to a few old timers, learned that it was easy to overlook silver ore when you were looking for gold. Besides, when mixed with galena ore (lead sulfide), which it is many times, you didn't know it was silver, unless it was assayed.

So Tom followed the veinlets and eventually ran into a massive lode of native silver and lead silver ore embedded in a contact zone between a granite intrusion and the limestone host rock. Chiseling out a sample from a four-foot vein, Tom sent a representative bag of crushed ore to a New Mexico chemist in Deming, and went back to work starting a tunnel on the side of the hill that was covered with ocotillo cactus. The chemist's report came to Tom at the hotel in Copper Flats with astounding news. The ore from the newly named Ocotillo Mine was very rich, running an estimated $750 worth of silver per ton. The lead was an additional forty to fifty dollars per ton. When he began to understand his good fortune, Tom decided to pay back his Dad for all the trouble he'd created. It never occurred to him that Dad didn't have the money, might not be interested in the deal, or might simply be distressed over his long-time absence.

Everything Tom said seemed to make sense. The tunnel revealed a substantial vein of silver ore and the assay report, signed by a professional chemist, sure indicated a commercial ore body. His sampling techniques were good, the vein appeared to get bigger as the tunneling proceeded and the limestone granite contact looked amenable for conventional mining methods. Tom had started to timber the mine entrance and planned on doing more, as soon as he could get the necessary oak from a few miles away. The only thing to worry about was running out of money before they could get ore to the smelter. With Tom's agreement, the brothers decided to make partial payment to Clyde and Mrs. Hurley; Dad had come up with $5,000, but wouldn't be happy if asked to pony up a second loan.

Neither of the Lawson brothers were big drinkers, but the circumstances demanded whiskey and a toast to the future. Ben would get things started in Ribera with buying wagons and mules, Tom would continue drilling, blasting and stockpiling the high-grade ore for delivery to Copper Flats. The Lawson family was about to get into the business of mining silver.

PROSPECTING

It took Konrad Bruner several days to adjust to his trip from Mexico and the stage coach ride from El Paso, Texas. The robbery, which had cost him his father's gold watch and fifty dollars in silver coins, had him wondering if coming to the New Mexico Territory had been a good choice. He'd heard stories about life on the western frontier, but until now, thought they were mostly exaggerations. The hijacking by the gang members made him realize that lawlessness was a fact of life. He also recognized how much he missed Old Mexico, the rich silver mines and the beautiful Luisa. "My gosh, that was an unbelievable goodbye from the finest girl I have ever met in my life." He had second thoughts about her constantly, but always came back to the same conclusion; conversion to Catholicism for him was impossible.

Part of his nostalgic feelings for Mexico was brought about by his comparison with Ribera. The town was in a very remote area where the closest town, Copper Flats, was over thirty-five miles away by horseback. To the west, Tucson was over one hundred miles away. There was a bank, general store, hotel and saloon and a livery stable, but not much else. People were generally friendly, but so far, no one had gone out of their way to develop a friendship with him. People were either too busy going about their chores, it seemed, of just didn't care about newcomers, especially from Europe. He was tempted to move on to Tucson, but decided that placer gold and a ride upriver might offer some possibilities.

Hiring a horse and saddle from Barney Pryor, he first rode downstream to look over Tent City, where several hundred miners were panning the river, hoping to hit pockets of gold granules and nuggets buried in the ancient riverbed. He was shocked to see the number of people working; tearing up the river bank processing the sand and gravel. Some were panning individually, others were in small groups using rockers to increase the amount of material they could process. To Konrad, it all looked very disorganized. His experience with placer mining was limited, but he couldn't make out where claims were boundaried and how they prevented overlapping. He stayed in the saddle observing the goings-on; in turn, they paid little attention to him. They were too busy moving around in the stream bed, hoping to find the nugget that would provide food and shelter for another week or so.

Entering Tent City, he saw a helter-skelter display of tar-paper shacks and canvas tents, some labeled as "food," "laundry," "bakery," and "saloon." One wooden building housed mining tools, cooking utensils, carpentry items and limited items of clothing. It was guarded by a bearded, mean-looking hombre who sat on a keg, holding a shotgun. The streets, ankle deep in mud, were strewn with garbage and leakage from several outhouses. The only semblance of civilization was Mrs. Galloway's bakery, which smelled of cooking pies and had chairs and a table on a platform, adjacent to her tent.

Gazing down-river, where most of the miners were at work, Konrad decided to move on, crossing the river on to River Bend Ranch property. As his horse scrambled up the riverbank, Konrad was halted by two ranch hands who shouted, "Hold on, Mister, just where do you think you're going?" The two riders were joined by Greg and Dale Newport, who had been inspecting damages to the riverbank. Before his father could acknowledge that he knew the German, Greg confronted Konrad rudely.

"I don't know who the hell you are, but this is River Bend Ranch land and we're damn tired of people messing up the river and the bank. If you're part of the Tent City rabble, it's time you respected private property." Dale Newport hastily intervened with, "Easy, son, Mr. Bruner is a newcomer to Ribera, probably just lookin' around, gettin' acquainted."

Ignoring his father's comments, Greg fired back, "Mr. Bruner, this river is the backbone of our ranch. We've been here over twenty years doing just fine without these damn miners. From now on, any attempt by anybody to disrupt the flow of water is declaring war on us and we ain't about to stand by and do nothin'. The sheriff has been sittin' on his hands for over a month, while these miners have pushed further and further onto our land. You can see the damage they've done." Getting more excited, as he talked, he looked directly at Konrad and spat, "You're new in town so let me give you some friendly advice. I understand you're some kind of mining expert, so I'd be damn careful working with these people. They could be real trouble for you."

Konrad waited for Dale to say something, but the elder Davenport remained silent. With that, Bruner frowned, tipped his hat and turned his horse towards town, thinking, "I feel sorry for Mr. Newport if that's the man who's in charge of his ranching operations."

Dale Newport was not pleased with his son's actions toward Konrad. He worried over Greg's hot temper and ability to offend people. "Sure, we got big problems with the miners, but why take it out on a stranger like Bruner?" Still, he said nothing to his son as they steered their horses homeward.

Back in town, Konrad paid a visit to Clyde Bond, thinking he knew as much about mining activity in the area as anyone. They talked about the river rising in New Mexico, then flowing generally southwest through Copper Flats and Ribera, before continuing into Sonora, Old Mexico. Clyde had explored the river a few miles past Copper Flats, but admitted, "That was years ago. I don't venture up that way much anymore, because I don't trust the Apaches since the army pulled out. There's no maps to speak of even though the country's been pretty well explored. Miners, prospectors and sourdoughs have criss-crossed the area, but those folks don't share good information very much. You'll find monuments all over the place. If I were you, I'd ride up to Growler Creek and look up Tom Lawson. He's been up there about a year; maybe he'll give you the lowdown on what's goin' on up there. Come to think of it, his brother was in here a few days ago looking for directions. Anyway, good luck; if I can help you in any way, come on back and see me. Who knows, maybe you'll find something worth assaying."

With his Brunton compass, pick, shovel and panning dish, Konrad led his riding horse and pack animal up the Bowie River. His trained eye observed rock formations on both sides of the river, which appeared to be the same. In some cases, thick vegetation covered parts of the banks, but overall, he began to get a picture of the regional geology. Moving methodically, he measured distances, chipped samples and recorded their location before bagging them.

On the second day out, he came upon the confluence of the river with Growler Creek, noting it was about twenty miles from Ribera. The creek was only a quarter of the width of the river, but flowed swiftly from the melting snows of Mt. Cody. He continued towards Copper Flats for a few miles, then retraced his steps and panned in several places that appeared to be possible collection points for gold particles. He didn't expect much, but bagged samples of sand and gravel for later examination. He then rode up Growler Creek, looking for an entry spot to Tom Lawson's prospect. Soon he found a trail from the creek that led to a spoil dump and the Ocotillo Mine. He was very surprised to see the ore stockpile, buildings and tunnel opening; it indicated a lot of work and, perhaps, an operating mine.

Ben Lawson called out hello and invited Konrad to come over and meet his brother. Initially, Tom was a very reluctant host, not interested in providing any information to the stranger. When he knew that he'd come into town on the same stage as Ben, he loosened up some. When Konrad began talking of silver mining in Mexico, Tom became relaxed and more cordial. The more they conversed, the more Tom and Konrad realized they had serious mutual interests. Tom told Konrad, "I came upriver some time ago. I was tired of the crowded river and wasn't doing much beyond enough gold dust to provide rice and beans. I stumbled on this by more luck than brains; I really didn't identify silver until I got the assay report back. I started punching a hole into the mountainside following the vein; now I guess you'd call it a tunnel. Here's a few samples of the native silver and lead silver ore, you can check them with the lab report to get a fix on things. Come along, let me show you what I've done so far and what I plan for the future."

As dusk approached, the Lawson brothers suggested that Konrad join them for some whiskey and water and a cowboy dinner of rice and beans. Over supper, the conversation drifted to Konrad's experiences in England and Mexico. As they learned more about Bruner's background, the Lawsons realized that Konrad could be a big help in developing the Ocotillo Mine. Equally impressed with the brothers, Konrad began to think that maybe this was the opportunity he was looking for. It was a fledgling operation that needed money and know-how to make it profitable. There were many unanswered questions, but most important, he trusted the Lawson brothers and decided to figure out a way to get an ownership position. After a good night's sleep, he decided he would approach them directly.

"Tom, I'm very impressed with what you've been able to do with your discovery. I believe the Ocotillo Mine has a lot of potential. I also believe I can help you bring this property to full production, not as an employee, but as a part-owner. Of course, I would want to review your sampling procedures, assay reports and do a general reconnaissance of the area. Most important, I'd want to verify that your claim has been properly filed." Felipe served Tom, Ben and Konrad flapjacks, bacon and coffee while they talked.

"I would visualize Tom staying in charge of tunneling, Dr. Ben handling the hiring of miners, working to pay off any loans and figuring out a way to economically ship the ore pile to the Copper Flats smelter. I would contribute by mapping of the area geology, delineating the orebody and forecasting reserves. I would also ensure that we get a fair shake on guaranteed recovery of silver and lead at the smelter." After receiving a statement of interest, Bruner continued.

"Let me dig into the details I mentioned, but based on what I've seen so far, here's my proposal: I would invest $25,000 for a 25% ownership in the mine and stockpiled ore. I would expect Ben to stay in Ribera for at least a year, until the mine is producing on a regular basis, so we are shipping ore to the smelter routinely, to generate cash. We'd discuss capital spending before making any commitments. That said, I believe we have the potential for a project that will benefit all of us."

Shaking hands, Konrad said goodbye to the Lawsons, promising to return in about a week. Both Tom and Ben were in a daze over Bruner's tentative proposal, but agreed that the German had made a very fair offer. They felt he would make a good partner and the plan would enable them to immediately pay back their Dad's $5,000 investment, if he so desired. The only thing that bothered Tom, though, was the thought of giving up a quarter of the mine to someone who hadn't been a partner when he made the discovery. The "seller's remorse" issue would continue to bother him for the next few days.

A LETTER TO NEW YORK

Peter Hillenbrand was bored and frustrated. He'd been in Ribera for almost three weeks and was pretty sure that there weren't any big business opportunities in the town or its surroundings. Ribera was growing, but three hundred people hardly qualified as a major population center. Days were hot and dusty; evenings surprisingly cool. He'd discarded all his city clothes for knee-high boots, dungarees and a western shirt, and learned to ride a horse, but had decided not to wear a gun on his hip; it could only invite trouble. He thought about a hidden revolver, but decided against a weapon. In any form. It plain scared him.

He'd visited Tent City a couple of times, but hadn't learned much from the miners or the owners of the saloon, restaurant, bakery and laundry. They seemed to be totally concerned with making as much money as they could, and fast, as sooner or later the gold would run out and the miners would move on. That was the pattern in California and western Arizona gold strikes and likely to be followed in Ribera. Any mention of the future and what was in store for the town and Tent City was met with a blank, silent stare. The diggings were giving up maybe fifty to sixty ounces of gold per week, but that was only an educated guess. Very, very few individual miners were getting rich; those that were, were keeping it a secret. Skullduggery, claim jumping and outright theft were rampant. The miners worked hard, digging sand and gravel every day, in water that was bitter cold. They left their ground only to go into town for supplies and equipment, sometimes even working Sundays. To Peter, it was a terrible existence.

His session with Brad Scoville, owner of the Mercantile Bank, hadn't shown much progress either. Brad revealed that he'd come down from Colorado ten years ago. The first few years were unpredictable, but he'd hung on as the town gradually increased in population. Most of his early loans were to ranchers; some had survived, but most had ended up selling out to the River Bend Ranch and the Newports.

Mr. Scoville had suggested a meeting with Dale and Greg Newport and had made arrangements for a dinner at the ranch. "PH" was pleasantly surprised with the sumptuous meal and red wine that was as good as anything he'd experienced in New York. While the dishes were being cleared, the men retired to Dale Newport's study for brandy and cigars. The room had a huge fireplace of fieldstone, in which a fire burned, providing illumination and warmth to the room.

Conversation was light and friendly until Greg Newport, on his fourth double, challenged the young New Yorker. "Well, Mr. Hillenbrand, you've been all around town asking all kinds of questions; just what in hell are you up to?" Taken aback, Peter looked at the group, but answered directly to Greg. "Greg, you're way off base. I'm simply on the lookout for business opportunities for my company in New York. With the war just about over, people and investment will be moving out this way. We want to be part of this growth; it's as simple as that."

Greg didn't like the answer. "Peter, that bullshit may sound good back East, but isn't going to cut it out here. You're up to something and I know it isn't going to be good for the River Bend Ranch." With that, he pushed Peter backwards, who tripped over a chair and fell to the carpeted floor. Both senior men helped Peter to his feet and apologized for Greg's behavior. Dale Newport told his son to leave the meeting, saying, "You've had too much to drink. Peter is a guest in this house and as long as I'm around, you'll not offend anyone who's been invited here. Gents, let's call it an evening; I'm sorry that things turned out this way."

Peter didn't mention the incident when he sent his initial report to the home office:

"Gentlemen: Last night, I had dinner with the Newports and Brad Scoville, who owns the Mercantile Bank of Ribera. The Newports own the River Bend Ranch, which is huge; it probably is over a hundred thousand acres and has a herd of about three to four thousand cattle. They also raise horses that are sold to the U.S. Army. The army, incidentally, is re-establishing forts between El Paso and Yuma, which should provide better protection for settlers and miners, who are coming here in increasing numbers. Mr. Scoville and the Newports asked a lot of questions about BM&G; I gave them the usual that 'we are looking for investment opportunities in the West, now that the Civil War is over.' They usually nod knowingly, but I can tell: they're suspicious of how it might affect them.

"Scoville and the Newports are the leaders in the community. Purely from a business standpoint, I would add Barbara Casey, who owns the general store in town. She's the widow of an army officer killed by Apache Indians a few years ago. She's probably in her late thirties and runs the store, assisted by her niece, who came out here when I did. Her store is the center of retail trade in town. She runs a good operation and I suspect is becoming a wealthy woman in the process. It's been rumored that she is looking to buy ranch property that is adjacent to Newport land. Mrs. Caruthers, owner of the land, has refused offers from the Newports. From what I hear, Greg Newport has warned her not to sell the property to anyone but the River Bank Ranch, but Agnes Caruthers is holding out, at least so far. The important thing about the Caruthers Ranch is that it is on the Bowie River, just north of town.

"Brad Scoville and Dale Newport appear to be close business friends and seem to quietly control things in town. Greg Newport is usually involved with day to day ranch operations, managing a crew of twelve to fifteen cow hands. Mrs. Newport stays busy running the farm, which grows corn, wheat, barley, oats and hay. The daughter and her husband help on the farm and handle veterinary work.

"Here is my summary of things at the present time:

"The bank, River Bend Ranch, and Mrs. Casey's general store dominate the local economy and will likely continue to do so in the future. Indians pose a threat to communities and loners between here and El Paso, but I get the feeling their influence is diminishing. I've barely met Sam Bellows, the sheriff; my impression is that he listens carefully to Scoville and Davenport Sr.

"Placer gold mining is an important contributor to the local economy. I have no accurate information on how much gold is being taken from the river, but it's probably in the range of fifty or sixty ounces per week. No one seems to really know. The panners bank some of the dust, send some home by stage coach and keep some for food and other supplies. There is very little credit given by the merchants; it's usually silver coins or gold dust at time of purchase, faces change rapidly here; people quit the river or sell out, which explains the cash demands of those supplying services.

"So far, the only lode deposits of gold have been north and west of here, over 150 miles away. I plan to hire Konrad Bruner, a German mining expert, to assess the extent of the placer deposits and how long they might last, assuming current production rates. I'll provide more information on Bruner later; he's worked in England and Old Mexico and is knowledgeable about precious metals.

"The general store is expanding in size and mix of products. Mrs. Casey is a hands-on manager and has an excellent supply base in Old Mexico, California and river boats that go up the Colorado River. Establishing similar stores in Copper Flats and Tucson would be a good conduit for goods from New England, to supplement existing suppliers. We could make an offer to purchase her store, but I will wait for your approval before I mention it to her.

"Banking would be a natural move for us and would be welcomed by the townspeople. They don't trust Scoville or the Newports because of past ranch foreclosures. If we were to build a modern bank with a secure vault, we could give Scoville serious, immediate competition. Town folk do business with Brad Scoville because he's the only bank in town, not because they like and trust him.

"The critical strategic issue in the area is water and who controls it. The Bowie River supplies the town and the River Bend Ranch, and so far there's been enough for all. However, the miners have disrupted normal flow from time to time and when that happens, tempers flare. I see trouble ahead because there isn't any government structure in place to mediate claims or force some sort of compromise. Both the miners and the Newports are well armed; it wouldn't take much of a spark to ignite a full-blown war between the two parties. Brad Scoville is actively searching for a compromise, but Greg Newport is spoiling for a fight. Sam Bellows, the sheriff, seems to be hoping the problem will go away on its own. I see real serious problems ahead here."

Peter posted the letter for the next stage and walked towards the general store. These periodic visits helped him to count the customers per hour, estimate the amount of each purchase and come up with a sales figure per day. It also gave him the opportunity to visit with Kate Hurley, the best-looking young lady in town.

He probably had a few weeks before he heard back from BM&G. Between now and then, he decided to talk with Konrad Bruner about the Tent City goldfields and study the transportation network between Copper Flats, Ribera and Tucson. He just might also find some time for a picnic with the lady from Tennessee.

Peter Hillenbrand's letter was well received in the New York office. Sam Batchelder was happy with the detailed report; maybe the young man was cut out for this type of work. The senior partner was particularly interested in the U.S. Army's re-establishment of forts and the supplies and equipment that would be needed. This was an important piece of intelligence. He decided he would contact General Harrison in Washington to see how the company could participate in re-stocking the forts and personnel in the West.

THE DRESSER GANG

Bart LaGrange lifted an eye open; the other one was puffed, closed and caked with dry blood. Vaguely, he remembered the stage coach robbery and getting clubbed by one of the gang members. Dimly, he recalled the face and features of his assailant, but couldn't place him. He was tied tightly, both hands and feet, when he received a sharp, painful kick to his ribs. As he squinted into the firelight, he could make out a group of five or six men, several of whom were dressed partially in buckskins. He could remember nothing that made any sense to him.

Their joking and banter were cut short by the voice of their leader, Major Benning "Turk" Dresser, a former Confederate cavalry office. The major was a graduate of West Point, class of 1858, who had elected to return to his home state of South Carolina when the Civil War broke out. Shortly after the second battle of Manassas, the Major had been wounded and captured, to spend the rest of the war in a Yankee prison camp. He'd survived the ordeal, but barely, living off rats, lizards and a variety of grubs and insects. After Lee's surrender, Dresser had gone home to the family plantation outside of Jacksonboro to find a heap of rubble and two stand-alone brick chimneys.

He learned that both parents were dead and a younger brother still missing. All slaves had left the plantation shortly after the Confederate surrender. Embittered over the turn of events, Dresser vowed to help rejuvenate the new Confederate Army and rebuild the family estate. Neither had happened, and Major Dresser degenerated to an ill-natured renegade, intent on robbing or destroying Federal property, particularly if a profit could be made. Nothing was off limits. Over a two-year period, he and his gang had committed numerous train robberies, bank holdups and attacks on wagon trains. Several of the outings included the murder of innocent civilians. As the federal government gradually restored order in the South, the Dresser gang moved steadily westward into Kansas, Arkansas, Texas and the New Mexico Territory.

Major Dresser ordered one of the men to cut Bart's bonds, and quickly he was jerked to his feet. Wobbling and breathing hard, LaGrange rubbed his wrists and hands to regain circulation in his hands. As he massaged his shoulders and neck, a large grizzled man stepped out of the shadows. Sizing up the foul-smelling individual, he cautiously recalled a member of the Kirkwood bang, named Tomber. Maybe his first name was Gus. It was the Kirkwood gang that had been badly shot up robbing the bank in Creosote, Texas.

As Tomber came close to Bart, he shook his fist, accusing LaGrange of complicity in the Wells Fargo ambush. "Major, this here guy is the one who ratted on us in Texas and got most of our gang killed. He got out of the fracas without a scratch; the only way that could have happened is that he was one of 'em. We got no business with this scum; he'll turn us in too if we give him half a chance." Menacingly, Tomber reached for his pistol, until restrained by the Major.

Fear rapidly shifted to opportunity as Bart LaGrange collected his wits. "Gus, you got it all wrong. I was still in the bank when Duke Kirkwood was gunned down with Jack Kimbrough. You guys were shooting your way out of town when I was slugged cold. Remember, I was the point man and didn't even carry a pistol. It all happened in a minute; when I woke up, I was held in custody by the bank detectives. Remember what I said: I wasn't armed. I haven't exactly been on a picnic since then either; you can take a look at my ankles and wrists and it'll tell you where I've been for the past year or so. I escaped from prison about a month ago. I'm a wanted man with a price on my head, so lighten up."

Tomber listened for a moment, then replied, "I never did trust you from the day I first saw you, and I ain't starting now. You was always buttering Duke up and he fell for your shit. Well, I don't believe your story one bit. You saved your own hide somehow and the gang got killed."

Turning to Major Dresser, he advised, "I'm telling you guys that LaGrange is bad news for all of us and we should shoot him dead right now."

While the argument was going on, Major Turk Dresser was listening intently to each man's story and had judged that the prison escapee's report had been the more believable of the two. He also picked up on Bart's mental quickness and decided that he might strengthen the gang's ability to hit the Bank of Ribera successfully. Turk was not pleased with his gang of cutthroats, who had no loyalty to the Confederacy, interested only in fattening their money belts. The gang believed they could storm any outback bank in the Territory and get away easily. Surprise and firepower were far more important to them than the Major's insistence on planning, teamwork and execution. They were ruthless and fearless, but poorly disciplined and inclined to look after themselves individually in a fire fight. As a cohesive, well-trained unit, they were simply second class. Gus Tomber, the hard-drinking quick-draw ruffian, personified everything that was wrong with the rabble.

While Tomber took a rest, Major Dresser walked to the center of the group and announced, "It looks to me that LaGrange did what anyone of you would have done under the circumstances. Think for your own safety, 'How can I get out of this mess?' Ain't nothing wrong with that, I'd say. We can use another gun for the bank job. We can keep a close eye on Bart; if he steps out of line or tries to escape, we'll take care of him on the spot." The gang looked at one another, shuffled their feet, and nodded assent. Still mad at the way things had turned out, Gus Tomber realized he'd been outsmarted by LaGrange, but vowed to get even with the man, at first chance.

Watching Gus walk away, Bart LaGrange knew he'd just had a close shave. He also knew that Tomber would be looking for a way to make him out a liar and possibly force a gun fight. He was an experienced man with a pistol, who wouldn't back off, even if it meant challenging the Major's leadership. Tomber would require constant surveillance and building a friendship with other gang members would be necessary. Turk Dresser's support would evaporate if he were to attempt an escape or reveal the slightest bit of disloyalty.

Overall, Bart LaGrange was not happy with his situation, but realized he would have to be patient. He had a price on his head, but had vowed that he would never return to Ft. Stockton and a sure, slow death. He wanted no part of Major Dresser's goal to raid the bank in Ribera, but knew he had to go along and bide his time for an escape opportunity.

Far more serious, his plan to "go straight" had again been sidetracked. Any return to a normal life would have to be postponed. He remarked to himself, "I wonder if I'll ever get the change to start a new life without crime. I seem destined to be an outlaw, always on the run."

He pondered these thoughts deeply as the Dresser gang saddled their horses for the ride to Ribera. As they doused their fires, two Apache warriors witnessed the departure and turned their ponies towards the Dragoon Mountains and camp.

WATER RIGHTS

The Bowie River rises in the weather-beaten mountains of southwestern New Mexico, flowing through southern Arizona, finally trickling into a shallow lake in Sonora, Old Mexico. It was the life blood of Ribera and its environs, providing drinking water for the citizenry, support for livestock and growing crops and vegetables. When gold was discovered in the riverbed, it created a new town, whose sole existence depended on retrieval of the yellow metal. Unique in desert country, the Bowie River flowed all year round.

For over twenty years, the supply of water was plentiful and unlimited and taken for granted by all. Farmers, ranchers and townspeople took clear water availability to be pure, unlimited and permanent. The River Bend Ranch, downstream from town, was the largest user of the river water, for cattle, horses and irrigated crops. Until gold was discovered, water rights and consumption were uncontested and free, for use by all. The discovery of gold in the riverbed began to modify this balance.

The stretch of riverbed adjacent to the River Bend Ranch was home to minute particles of gold that were hard to see with the naked eye. It usually required the prospector to swirl the sediments in a pan, hoping that the heavy gold particles would settle to the bottom of the dish as it's tilted and liquid is poured back into the water. Larger scale operations, using long toms or sluice boxes accomplished the same thing on a grander scale and were usually operated by several miners.

Prospectors from California had tested this alluvium and found gold in 1865. As word spread of the discovery, people converged on the river, staking claims and randomly scouring the sand and gravel. Minor strikes encouraged people to expand their activities, blanketing the area southwest of town. Their presence had little effect on the water supply for the town. It did improve the town's economy significantly as the miners bought tools, supplies and foodstuffs. A few major findings allowed for deposits in the Mercantile Bank that doubled, then tripled, the assets of the institution. When the Newports complained about miners trespassing on ranch land, Ribera merchants and Brad Scoville paid little heed. Sam Bellows, sensing that most people appreciated the commercial value of the miners, also did nothing to stop the encroachment of the diggers. He couldn't see where any laws were being broken; the river was there for everyone's benefit.

As news of the gold discovery fanned westward, more miners, merchants, hustlers and prostitutes moved in to establish Tent City and seek their fortune. Recently released war veterans and homesteaders also joined in the stampede from the east.

One cloudless, mild morning, while weeding her vegetable garden, Garland Newport observed murky, silty water entering her irrigation ditch. "Ain't never seen this before, I wonder what's going on." She called for Harry Rutton, the ranch foreman, to ride on down to the river and see what the problem was. Both Greg and Dale Newport were in back country rounding up stray cattle for branding. Harry saddled his horse and followed the dirty water to where the river normally entered the irrigation canal. As Harry approached the river, he could see that several miners were tearing down the riverbank, searching for gold. They were using picks and shovels, breaking up the sloping ground. Normally a serious, controlled individual, Harry exploded in a tirade of words. He pulled his pistol and fired two rounds in the air, yelling loudly, "This is River Bend Ranch land you're tearing up; you don't belong here. Now, get the hell off of this property before I start shooting at you."

Intent on their panning, at first the prospectors ignored Harry, which only infuriated the foreman. He fired off another shot close to the miners, which finally got their attention. As he closed in, one of the prospectors threw a fist-sized rock at Harry, hitting him in his shoulder and spooking his horse. One miner shrieked, "You don't own this goddam river; we got every right to be here. We're not moving. Get out of here before you get hurt." Rejecting Harry's pistol, the river men grabbed rocks and threw them at Rutton in a barrage that forced him to retreat. When two of the miners started towards Harry brandishing crowbars and shovels, he decided things were clearly out of hand and he'd better get help from the Newports. Spurring his frightened horse, he turned away from the miners and bolted for the ranch.

Hearing the shots, Garland Newport knew that something was going on at the river. Still, she was astonished to see Harry Rutton, beaten and bloodied as he reined in his mount at the main house. Painfully, Harry stepped out of his stirrups to be ushered into the kitchen, where Garland began to cleanse his wounds. "I followed the dirty water to the river, where the miners were tearing up the bank. When I approached them and told them to stop, they ganged up on me with rocks, picks and shovels. I fired the warning shots in self defense, then high-tailed it back here before they could get to me. I think those crazies were out to kill me, Mrs. Newport."

Believing the foreman's story, Garland decided to see Harry to his room for some rest, while she pondered what she should do next. She finally concluded not to report anything to sheriff Bellows until Dale and Greg got back home that evening. She also decided that it was time for them to confront the sheriff and get some action to stop the miners from taking over the river.

The following morning, the miners reached the riverbed to find a small army of heavily armed ranchers patrolling the banks where they'd been prospecting the previous day. A couple of the men were staking signs on the river's edge that read, "Property of the River Bend Ranch, no trespassing." As the signs were being hammered into the ground, Greg Newport approached the miners. "Let me be sure you understand these signs. Mostly for you guys that can't read—probably all of you–it says, stay off our property and stop tearing down the riverbank. This is a final warning to all of you. We're putting a stop to your invasion. The next miner that steps onto our land is going to get shot. And if you think we're not serious, just try us. I don't care what the circumstances are, if you so much as step on our land, you're gonna get a bullet in the head." The miners were mad at Greg's remarks, but knew he was also crazy enough to start a war. His show of force convinced them however to back off, get with Dan Sullivan and figure out a way to resume gold prospecting.

While the Tent City miners were meeting with Dan Sullivan to plan their next move, hands from the River Bend Ranch were busy building a small, but formidable, guardhouse close to the riverbank, where Greg Newport had issued his warning. The building was constructed of heavy timbers with gun ports that overlooked the active mining area.

With the resumption of clear water for irrigation, the guardhouse and frequent patrolling by armed ranch hands, peace was temporarily restored on the river. Sheriff Sam Bellows had been updated on developments, but knew that it was the lull before the storm. Greg Newport had issued an ultimatum to Dan Sullivan and the miners that wouldn't be ignored. Yet Bellows felt he could do little but warn both sides to stay within the law. And water rights weren't going to be clarified until Judge Bolton came into town, sometime in the next two weeks or so. He hoped both sides would relax, but feared that the miners wouldn't stay away from the river; it was their only livelihood. He knew it wouldn't take much to start a fight. This time, people were going to get killed.

Sam Bellows had met with Brad Scoville to see if he would talk with the Newports and Dan Sullivan. Scoville had listened to Sam, and replied, "I'm as worried as you are. Dale seems to have turned things over to Greg at the ranch and that's not good for any of us. You can't reason with Greg in a situation like this. I understand he's brought in a half dozen new hands that are probably nothing more than hired guns. Dale knows this, but appears to be going along with Greg. I can't figure Dale these days, he seems to have decided to fight, no matter what might happen. Dan Sullivan and the miners aren't much better. They feel they have every right to prospect the river and are not about to back down. Besides, Dan would just love to go head to head with Greg. Let's hope the judge gets here early this trip."

THE VOLUNTEER RANCH

The sun was up; the sky was clear and blue; it was going to be a good day. Ben Lawson bent over to pull on his knee-high, soft leather boots that were covered with dust. He sensed that Tom had something to say but was having trouble getting on with it. He waited calmly, knowing that eventually his brother would break his silence and speak. His patience was finally rewarded.

"Ben, I'm having second thoughts about Konrad Bruner's offer. I'm just not comfortable giving up 25 percent ownership to someone I barely know. Sure, he's worked in the English tin mines and old Mexico, but he's not family and hasn't done a lick of physical labor in the mine. I know Dad's $5,000 isn't going to last very long, but do we really want Konrad owning a quarter of the Ocotillo Mine?"

Ben knew that Tom was confused and wrestling with the issue of ownership. He'd consigned it to the "prospector mentality" and owning it all outright. He'd found the outcrop, started the tunneling and wanted full control, so he could make all the decisions and enjoy the full financial benefits of the property. At the same time, like others before him, he had no idea what it took to manage a mine or an appreciation for money requirements. He enjoyed the physical labor of drilling, blasting and mucking the silver ore, but had little taste for the administrative part of mine development. Ben also knew that his qualifications for either aspect of mining were very limited. Someone had to hire and train the miners, keep track of purchases and disbursements, maintain production and shipment data and keep records on a daily basis, in a journal. To the younger brother, Konrad was a gift from heaven. He knew geology, mine operations and smelting and viewed things from a long-term, broad perspective.

"Tom, Konrad has made you an offer of $25,000 for a twenty-five percent ownership position in the mine. That's roughly the value of the inventory on the ground. That money will enable us to start hiring miners, get them equipped and buy the supplies we need to continue production. We're also getting operational experience and a guy who will help in negotiations with the smelter people. I think it's a good deal all the way around. On the other hand, you're the man that made the discovery and has controlling interest, if we go ahead. You've put a lot of sweat into the mine and if you feel it's best to go it alone, we'll just have to figure on doing things a lot slower. It also means we'll have to use Dad's money. I'd like to help you decide, but Tom, it's your deal."

Tom was thinking hard, head down, running his fingers through uncombed hair. Finally, he looked at his brother and said, "I guess you're right, Ben. I don't know why I keep torturing myself. Let's go ahead with the plan for Konrad to buy in for twenty-five percent of the mine; you having twenty-five percent and me with fifty percent. If Dad wants to stay in on the deal, we'll give him part of our stock; if he prefers to get his money back, we'll settle up with him from Konrad's money."

Ben breathed a sigh of relief, hoping, but not expecting, that this would be the last discussion on ownership. He couldn't blame Tom; after three years or so of scratching around rocks and rubble, he'd finally hit something big. He was grateful that with such good fortune, he'd thought about his family.

When news leaked out from the lawyer's office and Konrad's bank deposit, people in Ribera began to take notice of the Lawson brothers' good fortune, Konrad Bruner's stake and activities at Growler Creek. Most folks were happy with Tom's discovery, though few had ever met the man or even seen him. A few jealously commented that "it was all dumb luck." Very few prospectors from Tent City packed their belongings for upriver; they were still transfixed on gold.

As official business manager of the Ocotillo Mine, Ben Lawson rode into town to settle past accounts and to buy new supplies. After getting even with Clyde Bond, he walked over to the general store, to see Barbara Casey. He'd decided to pay Tom's bill down in full, since the hiring of two miners required additional equipment and food. As he entered the store, he saw Kate Hurley talking to a couple of local ladies, examining bolts of cloth. She brightened, smiled and waved hello, conveying that she'd be with him in a minute or two. In the meantime, Ben found Barbara Casey and settled Tom's delinquent account. She was equally pleased when Ben placed an additional order with her. As she thanked him for the payment, Kate came over to join the conversation. As she joined them, Ben smiled and thought, "She sure is a fine-looking, pleasant lady; I should have my head examined for snoozing away my time on that stage ride from El Paso."

"Well, Mr. Ben, or should I say Dr. Ben Lawson, aren't you the modest one! Come to find out you're a medical doctor and now we hear that the Lawson brothers have a big silver strike up river." Briefly taken aback by Kate's familiarity, Ben recovered by saying, "Well, Miss Kate, this is the first indication that you knew I was alive, so I'll enjoy the moment. I have another errand to run, but I'd like to come back, if you'll join me for lunch at the hotel." He was being forward, but liked the girl and wanted to get to know her a whole lot better. Besides, he wouldn't get that many opportunities to get into town. When Aunt Barbara nodded, Kate told Ben she'd be ready to join him when he got back to the store.

Over lunch at the hotel, they shared growing-up stories and how they'd decided to emigrate to Ribera. Ben admired Kate's story on departing Tennessee and having the gumption to leave a comfortable, prospering farm for the desert of Arizona and told her so. Blushing slightly, she accepted the compliment. She was beginning to like this guy. As they were leaving the hotel, she explained that she was planning on spending a year with her aunt; business was booming and she needed the help.

"Interesting coincidence, Kate; I've promised Tom that I would stay on here for a year and help to get the mine up and running with him and Konrad. Maybe when you can get a day off, I'd like to take you up that way. It's beautiful country and you get a special view of Mt. Cody." She looked at Ben and replied, "I think I'd like that."

She was still embarrassed when she recalled her picnic date with Peter Hillenbrand. They had taken a carriage trip to the foothills of Mt. McCord, about six miles from town, to enjoy a picnic lunch of fried chicken and apple pie. After eating, Peter suggested a short walk to a creek that flowed in to the Bowie River. It was secluded, but Kate didn't give it a second thought; Peter was a gentleman. Sitting on a blanket by the water, "PH" moved closer to Kate and attempted to kiss her. She pushed him away, saying, "Peter, you're rushing things; I'm not going to kiss you, so please stop." Undaunted, Peter pushed Kate down on the blanket and clumsily groped for her breast, with "Come on, Kate, stop playing hard to get; let's have some fun. Besides, nobody's around." With that remark, Kate shoved Peter away, slapping him sharply on the cheek. She then stood up and walked rapidly to the carriage. After gathering the remnants of the picnic, she whispered, "Peter, I want you to take me home as quickly as possible. And don't bother with an apology; we won't be seeing one another again." Peter Hillenbrand realized he'd made a serious mistake, but still couldn't understand why the girl would go on a picnic six miles from town if she were such a prim and proper lady. "Women, I'll never understand them. Shoot, Colleen never acted this way, she was always happy to get in bed with me."

The trip back to Ribera was completed in silence. When Tom halted the team at Barbara Casey's house, Kate jumped down, grabbed the picnic basket and stormed off without a word.

* * * *

Barbara Casey had known Agnes Caruthers since her early days in Ribera. She too was an army widow who owned the OK Ranch and had moved there after receiving word that Master Sergeant James Caruthers had been killed in action. Mrs. Caruthers thought she could run the ranch with the help of one or two hands, but it became too much of a burden without her husband. After a sale of beef that barely covered her mortgage payment, she recognized that she was close to losing the property. Bonnet in hand, she approached Barbara Casey with her problem.

"Barbara, I'm not going to make it at the ranch; I've had some bad luck and I plan to rejoin my sister in Illinois. Things just haven't been right since Jim was killed. I hate to be a quitter, but it's time for me to move on. People don't seem to realize that the place is in a critical spot being on the river, north of town. I think the Newports have figured that they better protect themselves by buying me out. I don't like the way they do things, and most of all, won't give Greg Newport the satisfaction of bullying me on his terms. We've always gotten along well, so if you have any interest in buying a prime piece of land, here's your opportunity. Take over my mortgage obligations with Brad Scoville and for another thousand dollars, the OK Ranch is yours. If you can see your way clear in the next day or so, we can close before Greg is any the wiser. What do you think?"

Over supper with Kate, Barbara Casey brought up the subject of the OK Ranch and the visit from Agnes Caruthers. "I don't think you've met Agnes; she's been a good friend and really helped me when my husband was killed. Her place is north of town, on the river, with good pasture land and timber on the higher ground. She's tried to make a go of it without her husband, but it just hasn't worked out for her. She's decided to move back to Illinois, but doesn't want to sell out to the Newports. She stopped by earlier today to tell me her story and see if I might be interested in buying her out. The price for the ranch is very, very good. In fact, I'd up the ante so she can get a fresh start. If I were to go ahead with the purchase, I'd be antagonizing the Newports, but that's not going to stop me. Brad Scoville may not be too happy either, but I'm not going to worry there, either. Legal control of the river north of town has some interesting prospects. I told her I'd think about it and get right back to her. By the way, she feels that Sam Ortiz and his wife would be happy to stay on; both are good people and Sam is an excellent ranch hand. Betty can cook up Mexican food as good as anyone in the valley."

Kate looked at her aunt and offered, "Aunt Barbara, you've got a healthy, growing business here in town; why would you want to take on a ranch that is pretty run-down? It'll probably take two to three years to get it in shape. Assuming you have the money, where will you find the time to oversee the place?"

"Truth be known, Kate, my husband and I had a dream to eventually settle down and raise cattle and horses. His untimely death forced me to work in the general store and basically forget about ranching, at least for awhile. Secondly, Peter Hillenbrand came to me last week with an offer to buy the store. It seems his New York firm wants to get into retail distribution and plan to get started in Ribera, Copper Flats and Tucson. They would begin here by buying me out, rather than starting from scratch. They'd give me a down payment and make two more over a period of a year to complete the transaction. The store's been awfully good to me, but the possibility of becoming a ranch owner with land and water like the OK Ranch has an overwhelming appeal. The one thing that causes me to pause is thinking about how you would feel if I sold the store. I've learned to love you like my own."

Kate looked at her aunt and smiled with tears of joy. "Aunt Barbara, you know how much I like and respect you. Dad will be furious I suppose, but I'd love to help you get going with a ranch. It's what I've missed the most since leaving Tennessee. Between the two of us, we can manage the store and rebuild the Caruthers place. With help like the Ortiz family and a couple of hands, we'd be able to make a go of it. What do you plan on calling the ranch?" Barbara Casey grinned and exclaimed, "We'll call it the Volunteer Ranch, in memory of Lieutenant John D. Casey, U.S. Army, from the state of Tennessee."

When word leaked out that Barbara Casey had bought the ranch from Agnes Caruthers, Dale Newport fumed and reprimanded his son Greg for losing the deal. "You've been frettin' about the miners, and right under our nose that Casey woman walks in and steals the place. I thought you had this deal in your back pocket. What in hell went wrong?" Greg didn't answer his father right away, biting his lip. "Before you jump all over me, why don't you ask yourself why Brad Scoville didn't hold up the deal and let us know, before the sale went through?" Getting out-maneuvered by a couple of Army widows only added to the frustration of the moguls from the River Bend Ranch. What was their next move going to be?

A BANKER'S INTERVENTION

Brad Scoville was not a happy man. Things just weren't going the way they were supposed to. Nervously, he poured himself a double whiskey, gulped it down, then sat at his desk reviewing the events of the past week. He poured himself a second round of whiskey and drank it. His conversation with Dale Newport had gone nowhere; it almost seemed that his long-time business associate wasn't interested in seeking a solution to the river water problems. He was adamant on one point though; if Sam Bellows didn't stop the miners from digging out the banks of the River Bank Ranch, the Newports would take matters into their own hands.

What was most disturbing, Dale had delegated dealing with the problem to his son Greg. Questioned as to why he would do this at the time was met with, "Brad, just accept the fact that Greg is in charge and let it go at that." Whether he liked it or not, Brad had to face Greg directly, if there was any hope of a compromise settlement. Greg's hiring of six outsiders only confirmed that the Newports were serious in their intentions.

Gold production had fallen off considerably, as many of the miners held back from working their claims, but he knew that Dan Sullivan was biding his time, looking for a way to regain control of the river. Brad had also heard that the miners had received a large shipment of rifles and ammunition. Sure, the feud had abated, but Scoville knew that a renewed outbreak could happen at any time.

He'd also heard that Peter Hillenbrand was talking to Barbara Casey about buying the general store. By itself, it probably wasn't a problem. If it was a move to get involved with Mrs. Casey and the Volunteer Ranch, that could be a problem. He also had the premonition that the New Yorker was thinking about establishing a bank in the community. Hillenbrand's purchase of mining claims near Tent City only added to his agitation. "That damn kid is sure getting around," he murmured, as he tied his horse to a post near the main house of the Newports' ranch. He'd asked to meet with the Newports and Sam Bellows in hopes of delaying a fight between the rancher and the miners until the judge was able to render a legal opinion on water rights and ownership issues.

The hostilities between the two had reduced gold production and deposits normally made to the bank. He also worried that the importation of gun slingers wasn't a healthy sign that the town was well protected and secure. He was apprehensive that the $48,000 in gold in the bank's vault was a serious attraction to gangs, who always seemed able to get inside information on these things. Lacking confidence that Sam Bellows and his deputy were well prepared to handle any bank assault, Brad had decided to enlist outside help to protect his interest. Unfortunately, that help wasn't due to arrive for at least a week.

Garland Newport greeted Brad from the porch and ushered him in to the great room where Dale and Greg Newport were sitting, talking with Sam Bellows. There was a fire in need of wood in the fireplace, but still throwing off heat that felt good. As Scoville warmed his hands by the fire, Greg Newport stood up and said, "Well, gents, everyone's here, so let's get started."

Staring at Sam Bellows with teeth glaring, he got the meeting off to an unexpected rocky beginning. He challenged the sheriff with "Sam, I want you to tell me why Dan Sullivan isn't in jail and why you haven't kicked them damn miners out of the river for good. And don't give me some lame legal crap about sharing the river with those bastards. Forget your stock answer, just tell us right now, what you're gonna do to stop those tramps from destroying our river bank. The next thing you know, they'll be runnin' the whole damn town."

Sam shifted uncomfortably in his chair, slowly looking at the group. "Greg, you're losing sight of the fact that it was Harry Rutton who started the latest ruckus. If he hadn't fired off those shots, mostly likely we wouldn't be sitting here tonight. And bear in mind that Hillenbrand has legitimate claims south of the normal river flow, and needs water to work the gravels there. I don't see how a diversion dam, worked only in the daytime, is going to significantly disrupt water for the ranch. I've also assigned Buzz Chatham to keep tabs on things. If the miners do something illegal, he's authorized to make an arrest and put the people in jail. Things have quieted down. With your cooperation and help from the miners, I think we have the framework for a compromise." Turning to Dale Newport, Bellows added, "Dale, I'm due to meet with Sullivan and Peter Hillenbrand tomorrow. I think they'll listen to what I have to say about sharing water and avoiding any further trouble."

Before his father could answer, Greg flared up with, "Sam, you don't seem to get it! And what in hell is this talk about a diversion dam? I sure as hell haven't agreed to anything resembling a dam on the river. Sam, you better listen to me; I'm running things at the River Bend Ranch. You forget who put you in office in the first place and who's kept you there. I'm not here to compromise with the miners. We've run things in this town for the last ten to fifteen years and we're not giving up anything now. You get those vermin away from the river bank or we'll do it for you. We've got six new men on the ranch payroll who will help us clean things up if necessary. And I'll tell you, they know how to handle a shooting iron."

Sam Bellows glanced around the room, not seeing any dissent from the senior Newport. He didn't know why, but from now on, he'd have to deal with Greg Newport. When Brad Scoville appealed to Dale, his only comment was, "Boys, I'm out of the picture now. Greg is calling the shots and I support everything he's doing." As the meeting broke up, both Brad Scoville and Sam Bellows felt frustration as an opportunity to avoid an all-out war had evaporated before their eyes. Brad's intervention had failed.

THE BOWIE RIVER DAM

Attacking a huge breakfast of ham, beans and corn bread, Konrad Bruner was going over his field notes with Peter Hillenbrand. By trekking the Bowie River from several miles northeast of town, through Ribera and Tent City, he had mapped an area of several square miles. He'd also concluded that property adjacent to the present stream was a good prospect for placer gold. It would require extensive sampling, and if successful, the building of a diversionary dam. Properly managed, there would be plenty of water for the River Bend Ranch. As he showed Peter Hillenbrand his hand sketched map, "PH" questioned the potential of the tract. Konrad responded: "This is only an estimate, but it looks to me that the water you see today is a typical ox-bow river. If the river flowed where I think it did thousands of years ago, we could have something as big as the present diggings. The important thing is to tie up the land." He suggested that Peter check out who owned the claims on the land and if it were available at a decent price, buy them outright. If that didn't work, consider giving them a small royalty on ounces of gold pulled from the claims. Peter also agreed to a fifteen percent ownership for Konrad, based on geological work already completed and future exploration work.

Mulling over his conversation with the German, Peter Hillenbrand decided to take the plunge and invest his own money in the venture. This would be outside his employment agreement with BM&G. He didn't see any conflict of interest;

he was using his own money and since he was the one writing the reports, no one would ever be the wiser.

It didn't take Peter very long to gain full control of the land identified by Konrad as ripe for exploration. A few sold out, retaining a percentage of future earnings, but most were happy to walk away with enough money to move on to the next strike. Hoping to participate in the discovery of hard rock gold between Phoenix and Prescott, the men trooped northward.

Meanwhile, construction work began on a dam to divert Bowie River to a ditch entering Peter Hillenbrand's claims. A ranch hand from the River Bend Ranch, on horseback patrol, noticed silty water in the irrigation ditch. He rode far enough up the river to see dam construction in progress and decided he'd best alert the Newports. Turning his horse towards the ranch, he rode at breakneck speed to spread the news. When he told Greg Newport of the developments, Greg screamed, "This is it! If those bastards think they can steal our water, they're in for one helluva surprise. Buck, go find the old man. I'm on my way to check things out. If they're building a dam, it means war."

As Buck raced off to locate Dale Newport, Greg stormed over to the bunkhouse to get his men ready to take on the dam builders. Gathering Bill Lincoln, Chico Madero and three other hands, he inspected each rider to make sure they had a pistol, rifle, or shotgun and ample ammunition to make a decisive attack.

As the River Bend Ranch troop rode to the dam, Greg saw that the work was being supervised by Konrad Bruner and Peter Hillenbrand. Holding his men to the rear, he approached them and asked, "Just what in hell do you think you're doing?" Peter explained that he had posted claims away from Greg's ranch and intended to explore the ground for placer gold. He needed water to work the sand and gravel and it looked to him that a dam would allow all parties as much flow as needed. If they were successful, they would probably hire many of the Tent City miners and relieve pressure on diggings near the River Bend Ranch.

While Peter was explaining his position, Buzz Chatham rode up to see what the commotion was all about. Encouraged by the presence of the deputy, Peter went on, "We have a new plan for gold exploration that requires water away from the current river flow. The river's running full and we thought we'd take a portion for screening over here." As he pointed, Peter mentioned, "If we're successful, it will extend the life of gold mining in the community and keep a lot of people employed. These claims have all been properly recorded, so I don't understand what Greg's getting all worked up about."

Greg looked at Peter sharply and answered, "I'll tell you what I'm worked up about. We've been here for fifteen plus years and we're not about to give anyone water rights to build a dam. You push us dude and the next time you show up here, you better be packing iron."

"Hold on, Greg, that's not the way to settle things," asserted the deputy. "Let's see if there's some way we can stop the feuding." Greg grasped the situation and decided not to provoke a battle over the dam at this time. "Buzz, this problem has been simmering ever since the miners came to Tent City. The sheriff knows it and has done nothing to protect our rights. I'm telling you straight that we're through talking. The dam goes and we get our water back or we'll tear it down ourselves. We're fed up with Sullivan and his gang of carpet-baggers; they move one more shovel full of dirt from our banks and we'll be shooting, Buzz."

Before the deputy could anser, Greg turned to his men and shouted, "Okay, boys, let's call it a day." Sam Bellows would have a fit when he learned of today's encounter, but didn't have the manpower to create some sort of buffer zone between the antagonists. The answer was to get Greg Newport to cool down while something could be worked out. Maybe Brad Scoville could talk with Dale Newport alone. But Buzz knew that if Greg really was top dog, he would not accept any compromise and had the guns to back up his position.

As Greg rode into the main house area, he'd already made up his mind. "We're gonna clean out the miners from digging in the river bank and Hillenbrand's dam is going to be removed, one way or the other."

Meeting with his Dad later that evening, he carefully detailed the day's happenings. The elder Newport listened, asked a few questions, and finally said, "Well, son, I've let you down by trying to buy peace with the miners. They're riffraff that don't belong in this country and we're going to have to face it. The sheriff is a wimp, Scoville's banking more gold than he's seen in a lifetime, so it's up to us to straighten things out. I've spent almost twenty years working this place and I ain't about to see it threatened for lack of water. This ranch will be yours when I'm gone, so I'll respect whatever you want to do to protect it. One thing we have to do though, is decide, and take action. We're through pussy-footing around."

Shrouded by evening clouds that shadowed the moon, Greg Newport and Bill Lincoln quietly worked their way upriver to the damsite, which, surprisingly, was not guarded. Although water was flowing to the River Bend Ranch, new construction revealed a foundation for a future flood gate. They placed two kegs of powder at the base of the footing and left a trail of the explosive material of about eighty feet. Igniting the powder with a stick match, the sappers ran to their horses to escape the explosion. About a half mile from the damsite, they turned in their saddles to see the sky lit up in a massive detonation. The ground shook from the blast. "Well, Bill, that sure as hell sounds like a clear message to me. If that doesn't work, I've got a few more ideas to get the word across. Come on, let's call it a night."

Surveying the damage the following morning, Sam Bellows, Buzz Chatham and Peter Hillenbrand agreed that the culprits had done their job well. Peter commented, "Nobody has a monopoly on Bowie River water; that's the law. We both know who's to blame for the damage to the dam; we will rebuild and we expect to receive protection so it doesn't happen again. You can also tell the Newports that if necessary we'll bring in our own gunslingers, if that's what it takes." Sam Bellows suggested to Peter that he hold off until he'd had a chance to talk to the Newports, but received no agreement from the young man.

When Sam and Buzz rode to River Bend Ranch headquarters, the ranch looked perfectly normal. When he asked Greg Newport if he knew anything about the destruction of the dam, Greg glowered at the peace officer and smiled, saying, "Sam, I'm not admitting to a damn thing, but I'll tell you this: that water belongs to the River Bend Ranch and no group of bootleg miners are going to take it away from us. And that goes double for that kid banker from New York and the Dutchman. You want to avoid bloodshed? Good, tell 'em to quit building the dam or it'll happen again. We're not backing down, Sam, for any reason. If I were you, I'd get on with doing my job and stop trying to be nice to everyone."

Smarting from Greg's remarks, Sam knew he was between a rock and a hard place, with limited options. He knew the Newports had committed the crime, but had no evidence to support his claim. Fortunately, no one had been killed. He also knew that Greg would to it again if the dam were rebuilt. The Newports had taken on a new, demanding position that ruled out any middle ground. The hiring of the six newcomers only reinforced their commitment to control the river. Riding back into town, Sam decided he had to figure out a way to offset the firepower of the Newports.

His meeting with Peter Hillenbrand was even more disturbing. Peter insisted that the Bowie River water belonged to everyone and that an equal allocation of flow and a diversion dam was necessary to keep the peace. "Sam, we're not looking for a fight, but we're not budging; the law is on our side. We expect you to protect our rights. If you can't, we will do whatever is necessary to protect ourselves. The miners have had a belly-full of the Newports, and this time they aren't going to be bullied into moving. They are armed and will fight if necessary, to continue placer mining. It's their only source of making money. They have to make a living, Sam, it's as simple as that."

As the sun rose over Mt. Cody, Tom Lawson readied his shift crew to begin drilling and blasting for ore in the main tunnel. He was pleased with progress, but again, was re-thinking having Konrad Bruner as a partner. After all, he'd made the discovery, why had Ben been so fast to invite the German in to take a position in the mine? He'd have to talk to his brother again, before a final agreement was signed.

Twenty miles south of Growler Creek, a '44 rifle shot sent men scurrying for safety as construction began on the river dam.

Dan Sullivan traced the firing to an abandoned shack on River Bend Ranch land. With another miner, they covered the sniper on two sides and flushed him out with a barrage of pistol bullets. As the sniper ran for his horse, tethered to a nearby cottonwood, Sullivan took careful aim with his Volcanic .38 carbine and drilled the cowboy in the back with two shots. The killing was the spark that opened the war that the Newports were looking for; Dan Sullivan was a willing accomplice.

When Greg Newport got word that Marty Gimbel had been shot and killed by a miner, he organized his men to wipe out the construction gang building the dam. Half of his men would move up the river, while Greg's party would pass through the edge of town for a frontal assault.

Anticipating trouble, Sullivan and his men were well dug in and prepared for the fight. Whooping and yelling, Greg led his men into battle like a cavalry charge, to be met by a fusillade of well-aimed rifle fire. Greg and a second horseman were felled in the initial charge. The rest of the men veered across the river, seeking refuge by the Cimarron Cliffs, breaking off from the failed assault. The second group advancing from the south didn't fare much better. In broad daylight, rifle fire from the miners cut down two riders before the fight got underway. A third rider had his horse shot out from under him, crashing to the ground with a broken leg. A surviving ranch hand, recognizing the disastrous defeat, outflanked the damsite and rode at high speed to find Doc Gilroy and get help for the wounded men.

Galloping into Ribera, Rusty Jardine shouted, "Doc, there's been a fight at the river; the miners have shot up Greg Newport and his boys. At least five guys are dead or wounded and need your help right away. I'm going to ride and find Dale Newport, 'cause I'm sure Greg is one of them hurt badly." Kate Hurley, hearing the noise, joined Doc Gilroy to see if she could be of any help. "Kate, five men killed or wounded is damn serious. You can best help by getting up to Growler Creek, finding Doctor Lawson and telling him I need his help. And ask Barbara

Casey to get down to the river dam and give me a hand. We'll do the best we can until you get back."

Borrowing a horse from Barney Pryor, Kate hurtled up Main Street to alert Aunt Barbara to the tragedy and go after Ben Lawson. After two and a half hours of hard riding, she found Tom and Ben at the mine clearing. She explained the battle that had taken place and the number of casualties, and Ben grabbed his medical bag and raced for Ribera. Kate decided to rest her mount a while, before returning to town. Tom wasn't much of a talker and busied himself in the mine, but did have the horse watered and rested for Kate to return to town.

It was late afternoon before Dr. Ben Lawson reached Ribera. The town was in an obvious frenzy. Several of the town's citizens were heavily armed, a few were at the sheriff's office, shouting for Sam Bellows to jail the miners responsible for the bloodshed. Sam held the posse back, but they weren't willing to disperse. The crowd wanted revenge, even though they'd only heard one side of the story. The miners were still at the damsite, patrolling the area, though work had stopped. Buzz Chatham had gone to the river, but as yet hadn't returned with any additional information.

Meanwhile, Doc Gilroy worked feverishly to help the wounded. Two were seriously hurt by rifle fire, but with luck and no infection, would survive. Two others were in the back room, being tended to by Barbara Casey and another lady; they would be all right in a week or so.

Greg Newport had been shot three times and was in critical condition. Gilroy asked Ben Lawson to look over his patient to see what they could do about stopping the bleeding. Doctor Lawson went to work immediately, tying off torn arteries and veins, probing for a third bullet that Gilroy had been unable to locate. Doc marveled at the speed of Ben's first aid for the wounded man. Unfortunately, his efforts were futile and the young man died while his sister and mother looked on helplessly.

Working as a team, the doctors finished patching up the wounded and left for a breather at the Whitman Hotel saloon. It had been quite a day in the life of Ribera. That evening, Dale Newport arrived in town to view the body of his only son. Head bowed, Dale asked where he could find Peter Hillenbrand. No one seemed to know. Sensing that people were protecting the New Yorker, he walked up Main Street to the jail, assuming that he was being held there by the sheriff.

Sam Bellows knew that the death of Greg Newport meant big trouble. His father was an important man in town, and very much inclined to have his way with things. It didn't seem to matter whether it was lawful or not. Nevertheless, he was not prepared for the rage in Dale Newport's eyes when he stormed into the sheriff's office. "My son's been gunned down in cold blood by a bunch of hooligans and you two are sitting here slopping up coffee. What the hell kind of people are you? Hillenbrand and Sullivan should be dancing at the end of a rope."

"Dale, we don't know for sure who started the shoot-out; all we know is that we have one dead person and four or five more wounded. Buzz has talked to Hillenbrand and the miners; their story's a lot different from what we got from your boys. We'll get to the bottom of things tomorrow. Don't try to take the law into your own hands, 'cause I'm not going to let you." Dale Newport reached for his sidearm, still believing that Hillenbrand was in custody at the jail. In an instant, Buzz Chatham hit Newport on the side of his head with a nightstick; the rancher slumped to the floor, unconscious. They dragged the senior Newport to a jail cell and anchored his hand to a metal cot for the night.

The sun came up to a hushed Ribera. Doc Gilroy visited his makeshift hospital to see how his patients were getting along. After a brief examination, he chatted with Barbara Casey and Kate Hurley. He decided that the wounded would live, thanks to Ben Lawson and his surgical skills. "I'd no idea how battlefield medicine had progressed so much in the war. Lawson's instructions on infection prevention and control were particularly noteworthy. That's one, and the only, benefit I can think of that came out of the Civil War." As he walked to the jail to check on Dale Newport, he thought, "Boy, we could sure use a doctor like Ben Lawson in this town." After watching Dr. Lawson for a good part of the night, Kate Hurley agreed, but for another reason.

A SUNDAY RIDE

Ribera was usually quiet on Sunday mornings; shops were closed, people went to church, ranch hands were sleeping off their Saturday night carousing. A few of the revelers woke up in jail, escorted there by the sheriff and his deputy for excessive rowdyism the previous evening.

Ben Lawson saddled the paint he'd gotten to like, and headed up Main Street to join Kate for a Sunday ride. As he reached Mrs. Casey's house, he noticed two saddled riding horses and a pack animal, loaded down with kitchen equipment, carpentry tools and foodstuffs.

"Ben, we have a guest who'd like to join us to the Volunteer Ranch. I told Aunt Barbara that we'd love to have her company; you haven't seen the ranch and she'd appreciate your opinion on a couple of things. I didn't think you'd mind, Ben." The doctor nodded with "Of course, it's good that she can join us," while thinking to himself, "I thought we were past the stage where we needed a chaperone." Kate had a wide-brimmed hat on that covered most of her dark brown hair, which was tied in a pony tail with a bright pink ribbon. She wore a white cotton blouse with a red bandana around her neck, riding jeans and tan, polished riding boots. When she smiled, Ben blushed; she was the prettiest girl he'd ever seen.

Ben had hoped for a day of sunshine and blue sky so he and Kate could continue their ritual of getting to know one another. He was disappointed that his dream wasn't meant to be, but concluded that just being with Kate was enough, for the moment. Besides, he liked Barbara Casey and wanted her to like him. He wanted her on his side.

The threesome moved up the Bowie River towards the ranch, Barbara explaining that Peter Hillenbrand and his bank had made her an attractive offer on the general store. She intended to accept the proposition, pending an approval from her son. "I sent Tom a letter, asking for his thoughts on the idea of my leaving the store; I expect he'll tell me to do what I think is best. He's so much like his father; serious, very thoughtful, but very independent. He's also a dyed-in-the-wool Union Army soldier, who will be commissioned at West Point this June and is looking forward to a career in the cavalry. Kate has encouraged me to sell the store, so I really can't come up with a good reason not to sell, close out my career as a storekeeper and become a full-time rancher. How does all this sound to you, Ben?"

"Barbara, I don't know that much about your business, but if the Volunteer Ranch will keep your niece in Arizona for a while longer, I'm all for it." The aunt responded with a knowing wink of her eye that said, "I like you two."

As the ranch house came into view, Ben was silently trying to figure out how the sale of the store might affect Kate's future in Ribera. Was she getting tired of the town, was she bored and anxious to get back to Tennessee or was she going to stay on and help rebuild the old Caruthers place? Maybe she had a boyfriend back home, waiting for her.

The ranch house was located at the base of a gradually sloping hillside that was covered with clutches of prickly pear and cholla cactus. It faced towards the Bowie River which was about a mile and a half to the East. A sturdy looking barn had been fashioned from fieldstone and appeared to be in good condition. The corrals looked a little tired, but were being fixed up by Sam Ortiz, Barbara's first hired hand. He greeted them with a warm "buenos dias" as his wife waved from the porch of the main house. They dismounted, tied their horses to a hitching post and made their way to the kitchen where Betty Ortiz had cooked up a solid fare of beans, squash and beef enchiladas. Fresh salsa added color and taste to the luncheon.

The main house, though small, had been worked on recently and showed signs of improvement. One of Barbara's first ideas was to expand the main house, get the corrals repaired and deepen the well for drinking water and for the animals. Ben immediately took a liking for Sam and Betty Ortiz; they were friendly and talked knowledgeably about the ranch and plans for the future. Sam was a short, stocky man with large, rough hands that had experienced years of hard work.

After the meal, Barbara led them on the trail to the river. Standing at the confluence of the Bowie River and Growler Creek, she commented, "You can see why the Newports wanted this place; I've probably got two miles of river front, fairly close to town and unlimited access to water. If the town continues to grow as it has in the past, I can see myself even selling a few building lots." Gazing down the river, they saw a lone prospector who was totally absorbed in panning and sampling. Hearing voices, the man turned, waved hello and shouted, "Hello, Ben; what are you doing up this way today?" Ben returned the signal, recognizing the German in his broad-brimmed cowboy hat.

Removing his hat, Konrad walked towards the group and introduced himself. After a brief chat about the river, Barbara invited Bruner to join them for dinner at the Volunteer Ranch. Betty Ortiz again served up an excellent meal as Konrad talked about his experiences in England and Old Mexico. Ben joined in reviewing their partnership in the Ocotillo Mine and home life in Colorado. As he mentioned his father, he realized how far away he was from practicing medicine and wondered if he would become a mine operator with Tom, or eventually return to being a doctor. In the past two months, the only doctoring he'd done was after the fight at the damsite. As he daydreamed, he thought of Kate Hurley and how she had become the center of his universe. She was unlike any woman he'd ever met. In his musing, comparing mine operations with being a doctor, he realized that whatever choice he made, Kate Hurley had to be with him. At that moment, she looked up at Ben and both smiled at each other.

After dinner, Barbara took Konrad on a tour, while Ben nervously suggested to Kate that they step outside to view the sunset. Kate adjusted a shawl around her shoulders and, looking directly at the doctor, whispered, "Ben, I'm sorry the day got a little crowded, but I didn't think you'd mind. Barbara is so excited about the ranch and with Sam and Betty Ortiz here, wants to get a good head start on things before winter sets in." As she smiled, Ben softened. "Kate, any time I can spend with you is a real pleasure. I just want to get to know you better. If you feel we need a chaperone when we're together, that's okay by me." Kate laughed and putting her arms around Ben's neck, exclaimed, "You poor dear" and kissed him on the cheek. With that encouragement, Ben held Kate closely and kissed her on the lips. Both hugged one another and held on tightly as Barbara Casey and Konrad returned from their walk. Releasing themselves from their embrace, they held hands, savoring the experience as the sun slowly faded into dusk.

The foursome rode back into town as darkness approached. After the women were escorted to Barbara's house, Ben and Konrad sat and chatted in the lobby of the hotel. "Ben, we're having a few problems at the mine we should talk about. We've hit a barren zone that is practically void of silver. I'm pretty sure it's a fault zone where the granite and limestone are in contact. There's been some slippage, which is to be expected in structures like this. I think I can figure things out if I study the strata and determine which way the wall rock has moved." Ben nodded; he really didn't know what Konrad was talking about, but it sounded good. "I may need your help in talking to Tom. He's upset with the ore grade falling off and is raising hell with the Mexican miners to work faster. It's not their fault; they can't move the gangue any faster. Once I know which way the limestone has shifted, we'll be all right.

"More important perhaps, we've lost high grade ore from our stockpile. I don't think it involves our guys; it's most likely someone from the border. I've checked the pile for the past few days and without question, we've lost ore. We've got to come up with a way to prove that we're losing stuff from the pile. It appears that we're being robbed at night, when everyone is asleep. Sheriff Bellows and his deputy are tied up with the feud over the river water, so we can't count on them for any help. You got any ideas?"

Ben stroke his chin, replying, "Konrad, we had similar problems in Missouri at times. I may have an idea that will help us identify our ore after it's been stolen. I'll check with the assay office tomorrow and get us set up before nightfall. I'll let you know when I get back if I've gotten what I need."

Konrad was curious as to what Ben had in mind, but kept his inquisitiveness to himself. He could wait until tomorrow for an answer. As they decided to call it a night, Konrad remarked how nice it had been to have a good home-cooked meal in the company of two very attractive women. "I could get real interested in a person like Barbara Casey. She's smart, friendly, and I think could learn to like me. I've got to spend a little more time at the general store, Ben." Ben only grinned and said, "Me too, Konrad."

BM&G MAKES A MOVE

Peter Hillenbrand read the letter a second time to be sure he understood the instructions from the New York home office. George Batchelder, senior partner of Batchelder, Monroni and Gable, had signed the memorandum, instructing Peter to "proceed with dispatch" to purchase Barbara Casey's general store. In the total scheme of things for the firm, the buying of a general store in Ribera, Arizona, didn't amount to a large amount of money, but certainly was a new direction for the investment bankers. It also placed a lot of responsibility on the shoulders of Peter Hillenbrand. His initial reaction was positive; on the other hand, it could mean he would be involved in similar purchases or start-ups in Tucson, Copper Flats and El Paso, Texas. "I'm not sure I want to spend the next five or ten years in the blistering heat of the Sonoran desert, living on the frontier." Reviewing his immediate options, though, he decided to follow Batchelder's instructions and worry about the long term later on. It could be worse; they could have decided to have him actually run the store.

It fell to Peter to evaluate the worth of the building, value the inventory and add twenty-five percent of the total to arrive at an offering price. A third of the sum would be paid at closing, a third after six months and the final third after a year's operation. Mrs. Casey would be required to stay on as manager of the store for a six-month period, to train a replacement supervisor. This person would be hired by the home office and be on his way to the Territory, once the purchase contract had been signed. The final suggestion was to get the offering closed as quickly as possible.

The letter also told Peter to move ahead on establishing a banking presence for BM&G in Ribera. Later, they would build or buy banks in El Paso, Tucson, Yuma and San Diego. In considerable detail, Mr. Batchelder explained why the company was convinced that these towns would eventually grow into cities, as a railroad was built across Texas, the New Mexico Territory into California. The federal government would help build this railroad and attract settlers to the area by offering cheap land, subsidizing irrigation projects and encouraging mineral exploration. Indians would be moved to reservations as white people moved in to ranch, farm or prospect. Washington had every intention of strengthening its southern border and discouraging any idea that Mexico might have of regaining their former northern properties. Those investors who joined early in this development would be rewarded handsomely.

Peter spent the next week examining Barbara Casey's store procedures, inventory and establishing methods to add new shipments and delete sales. Overall, he was impressed with Mrs. Casey's controls in running the business. He spoke extensively with Harry Cartwright, owner of the Whitman Hotel, regarding real estate values, and consulted with several others about sourcing of food and equipment. When Fort Gore was fully staffed, he made estimates of their requirements. He did all this, carefully avoiding any direct contact with Brad Scoville, who nevertheless received reports regularly on Peter's activities.

With an inventory finally fixed, Peter added his estimated value of the land and buildings, adjusted the number by twenty-five percent for good will, and came up with a sum of $36,000. Shocked, Hillenbrand reviewed and double-checked his figures, finally deciding to follow instructions and allow the $36,000 figure to stand.

He also decided that with luck, his gold prospecting would begin to pay off and give him the personal wealth he desperately wanted. He'd worry about an explanation of his side activities to the firm if and when he submitted his letter of resignation. In the meantime, he'd give his full attention to closing on the purchase of the general store.

When Peter entered the general store, Kate Hurley turned away from him and asked Barbara Casey to see what he wanted. Any possibility of striking up a new romance with the young lady was clearly only wishful thinking. Meeting with Mrs. Casey, he explained he had a formal offering, so they retreated to an office in the warehouse, behind the store. He showed her the offering; with little hesitation, Barbara accepted the proposal by initialing each page and signing the final sheet. "Your idea of keeping me on for a six-month period to train a new manager is good sense, but I also expect to be paid for this activity. I believe $300 per month would be a fair wage."

Peter accepted Barbara Casey's suggestion and told her a check for $12,000 would be forthcoming within thirty days representing a closing payment for the business. After a handshake, Peter left the general store and went to the hotel to catch the next outbound mail. For the first time since arriving in Ribera, Peter was pleased with himself on making his first deal. He would have been a lot happier if he had decent female companionship to share it with.

He had a distinctly different feeling when he left Brad Scoville's office several hours later. Or, perhaps getting thrown out of the banker's office would be a more accurate picture of what took place.

Brad Scoville was well aware that Peter Hillenbrand was up to something; he wasn't sure of just what. He knew he'd been talking to Cartwright about real estate values; that in itself didn't worry him any. He didn't believe a New York Investment banking firm would have any serious interest in a retail operation like the general store. A little more confusing, "Where did Hillenbrand's involvement with Konrad Bruner in placer gold fit into the picture?"

Unaware that Peter Hillenbrand and Mrs. Casey had agreed to a sale, he laced into Peter as soon as he entered his office. "Just because you have Eastern money behind you, don't think for a minute you can waltz into this town and buy anything you want. You may think Barbara Casey might sell out to you, but believe me, she wouldn't do a thing without talking to me or Dale Newport. We've run this town for over ten years and we're not about to turn things over to someone like you. Furthermore, don't get any ideas about me selling this bank. I've worked hard to build up what I've got, and I ain't about to give it away to you guys. Do you really think you can steal my depositors away with a new bank? You'd better think again, young man."

Stunned, Peter could only reply, "Mr. Scoville, I'm sorry you feel that way." Before Peter could finish his sentence, the banker glared at him and blurted, "I've seen and heard enough of your actions, just get the hell out of my office and don't come back. Good day, sir!"

Peter was disappointed with Brad Scoville's tirade and was at a loss to explain why he was so riled up. "What the hell will he do when he hears that BM&G has bought Barbara Casey's store?" He sure sounded serious about not selling the bank, even before he had received an offer. Peter decided to write the home office, explaining today's episode, and suggesting building a bank from the ground up would probably be the best way to go. A new state-of-the-art security system and vault would give them a strong competitive advantage.

As he posted a second letter for the day, he waved to Barbara Casey as she walked by. Noting her attractive smile and stylish figure, he mused, "I wonder if Barbara Casey would be interested in a little courting. She's sure friendly enough; she may have a few years on me, but heck, so did Colleen. Plus, she doesn't seem to have any male company that I can see. I think this bears looking into a bit."

COPPER FLATS

Konrad Bruner and Tom and Ben Lawson surveyed their ore stockpile and, after some discussion, concluded that their inventory was indeed shrinking. As they looked around the minesite area, they decided that most likely, the ore was being stolen at night and transported south by using an old trail that reached to San Sebastian, Old Mexico, over thirty miles away. A half dozen thieves with strong backs could easily account for the missing ore over a period of two weeks. They determined that two to three tons of high grade ore could add up to three thousand plus dollars, since some of the material was almost pure silver. The owners debated how to deal with the problem, finally agreeing to talk to the sheriff before taking any serious action. Tom was all for arming a few Tent City miners and shooting first, then asking questions, but finally agreed to the legal approach preferred by his brother Ben and Konrad Bruner.

Ben wasn't too surprised to find Sam Bellows only mildly interested in the problems at the Ocotillo Mine. "You men are twenty miles from here; I've got one deputy and he's tied up trying to keep a lid on the Tent City boys. We've got to avoid another firefight on the river and it won't be easy; the Newports are enraged over the death of Greg. You might want to talk to Sheriff Mike Timmerman in Copper Flats; he's got things pretty much under control up there."

Leaving the sheriff's office, Ben walked down Main Street to enter Barbara Casey's general store. Several miners were looking at boots and clothing, also trying to cozy up to Kate Hurley. Barbara came from nowhere to engage the miners, while Kate greeted Ben. She was dressed in a long, checkered, blue gingham dress that revealed a well formed body and small waist. Ben acknowledged to himself that "she sure is a pretty thing." With a bright smile, Kate showed the doctor new pots and pans, a Dutch oven and utensils that would help establish a kitchen able to take care of a dozen men at the mine. She also suggested "we take a ride out to the Volunteer Ranch this Sunday, this time without a chaperone. Barbara will be busy on the new construction going on; we could have a picnic by ourselves." Ben stammered a "Great. I'll be by your place around noon. I'll have a buggy this time," as he floated out the door of the store. Riding back to the mine, he decided he really loved that girl. They'd met only twice, but in his heart, he knew she was the one.

He found Barney Pryor at the livery stable, cleaning stalls and feeding the horses. Explaining that he needed heavy duty wagons and mule teams to haul ore from Growler Creek to Copper Flats, Barney countered with an offer to handle the whole deal. "Ben, I 've been looking for something like this for quite a while. I've got wagons and mule teams; I'll hire a couple of skinners and that should do it. I will charge you $6.50 per ton of ore to take it from the mine to the smelter, providing you give me space near the mine where I can build a shed and corrals for the mules. You also have to give me all your business for a year; after that, we'll sit down and decide on a permanent contract. I'll keep good records that we can review together periodically. I like what I see with you fellers and see this as a good deal for both of us. Give me a couple of weeks to get the young Cruz kid trained to run things here and I'll be ready to go."

Ben was more than satisfied with Barney's offer, deciding he would be a good transportation partner for the mine. Now to find a few more good reliable miners and have them move to Growler Creek. On the way out of town, he stopped at the assay office to purchase two large cans of green paint, the only color Clyde Bond had in stock. Bond raised his eyebrows at the buy, but Ben decided to keep what it was to be used for to himself.

When he got back to the mine, Tom and Konrad were discussing the next phase of drilling, blasting and removal of the ore from the face of the tunnel. The original vein was holding at about ten feet in thickness, but native silver was diminishing and lead ore (galena) was increasing in content. The fault zone was almost barren of either lead or silver ore and distinct, in that the rocks had been ground up, composed of fragments from the granite and limestone encountered previously. Konrad wanted to stop and study the situation, concentrating on broken ore removal; Tom wanted to dig through the softer material in hopes of finding the original vein again. They compromised; ore removal would slow down appreciably, while Konrad studied the stratigraphy and geologic structure around both sides of the fault. While this was going on, Ben decided to visit the sheriff in Copper Flats and meet with Les Ventor, superintendent of the local smelter.

Ben rode into Copper Flats in the early evening, listening to the tinkling of a pounding piano at the Empty Saddle Saloon. Ordering a beer at the bar, he glanced to a card table where four well-dressed men were playing poker. Close by were a few dancing ladies and what looked to be a group of smelter workers. Asking the barkeep if Les Ventor was about, the reply was, "No, you won't find him here at any hour; he's a family man who tends to keep to himself. He has a small ranch a few miles out of town; but it would be best to just show up at the ISC smelter first thing in the morning; any time after seven o'clock."

After leaving his horse at the livery stable, Ben checked in to the Galena Hotel for a quick meal. In his room, he reviewed the day. The agreement with Barney Pryor had been a pleasant surprise, but differences between Tom and Konrad seemed to crop up all too often. Tom was obsessed with getting money out of the mine; Konrad wanted to proceed cautiously, studying the rock structure and making certain that safe working conditions were being maintained. He was adamant in explaining that safe working conditions were required to protect good workers; they also fostered high productivity. They had experienced no accidents and Konrad was insistent that proper timbering be in place before new tunneling went forward. Tom, on the other hand, was willing to cut corners to speed up production. In the process of debating this issue, Ben felt that his brother still hadn't accepted the idea of an outside investor. The fact that Konrad could be stubborn at times only tested relations further. It had been a long day; answers to these questions would have to wait for another time.

Noise from the main street and noxious sulphur fumes from the ISC smelter awakened Ben early. He rapidly washed and breakfasted and was at the smelter a few minutes after seven o'clock. Les Ventor was a professional metallurgist who'd received his early training in Idaho and Montana. He was a full partner in International Smelter Company (ISC) and was very interested in adding additional production to his plant. Most of the current ore was lead sulfide (galena); with minor amounts of Zinc sulfide (sphalerite); the prospect of processing a higher value ore was welcome news.

Feeling comfortable with their conversation, Ben strolled down Center Street to find the sheriff's office. The smell of fresh coffee took him to the jail, where Mike Timmerman and his deputy Titus Mallory were studying new "wanted" bulletins. The names of Turk Dresser and Bart LaGrange were prominent among the fugitives listed, each with a posted reward. Dresser was considered armed and dangerous and sympathetic to rebel guerilla activities; LaGrange was described as "escaped from the state prison at Ft. Stockton, Texas." Dresser's capture, dead or alive, had a $2,500 reward; Bart LaGrange's capture was worth $1,000.

Ben explained his position as partner in a newly opened silver mine at Growler Creek and the importance of delivery of ore to the ISC smelter.

"Look, Mr. Lawson, I can tell you that your stolen ore ain't comin' here to the smelter. Even if it did, Les Ventor would tell us about it and we'd grab the crooks. My guess is it's going south around Mt. Cody to the gypsy smelters in Mexico. If we see any strange Mexi's up here, we'll let you know about it, but your best bet is to hire a few people who are handy with weapons to guard your mine and delivery wagons. Once those wagons get to Copper Flats, they're safe, I can tell you."

Frustrated, Ben was slowly realizing that southern Arizona was wild and peace-keeping was minimal. Sheriffs might break up bar fights and enforce local laws, but avoided problems outside of town, if they could. They did their best to protect the banks and keep an eye out for fugitives on the lam, otherwise they weren't interested in some guy's mine out in the brush ten or twenty miles away. He'd have to figure out how to protect himself. To expect anything more than that was pie in the sky thinking. Ranchers fought settlers, miners trespassed on private property (however defined) and disputes were settled man to man with knives, pistols or rifles. How a town eventually became safe to live in was a mystery to Ben Lawson.

The ride back to the Ocotillo Mine took him past the Volunteer Ranch and the thought of next weekend's trip with Kate Hurley. He knew she was interested in him; he just hoped it was serious love and not just a casual infatuation. Maybe he'd bring her a small gift on their Sunday picnic, but off hand, he couldn't think of anything besides wild flowers.

As he approached the mine, he heard Konrad and Tom arguing over production rates and work conditions in the mine. Konrad was pleading with Tom to ease up on production, but Tom wasn't agreeing with him. This time, Ben decided to let them argue until they reached agreement their way, on their own, whatever way that was.

Now that they had a cabin with bunk beds and a stove, living conditions were improving. The cook had fixed a venison stew, sour dough bread and spring water coffee that helped quiet things down a bit. Breakfast was equally peaceable, with conversation directed toward poaching and how to deal with that problem. Ben wasn't happy when he was elected the person to protect the ore pile and see that deliveries were completed safely, but grudgingly admitted that he was the likely candidate. He knew the law enforcement people, had contracted with Barney Pryor on transport and was in the best position to hire guards or gunslingers, as necessary. He also knew it was time he became familiar with shooting a pistol; he just might need it, to stop the poaching.

* * * *

Toasting one another with hearty laughs, Castro Diaz and Rusty Dillon swallowed their second tequila, celebrating their heist of the silver ore from the Ocotillo Mine. The Vaquero Cantina was their hideaway after the ore was taken from San Sebastian to the rogue smelter, who serviced many small gopher hole operations in northern Sonora. Rusty Dillon had teamed up with the Mexican after hearing about the strike of high grade silver by Tom Lawson. He was tired of groveling in the river and missed seeing his girlfriends at the cantina. This was a much easier way to make a living and a lot more fun. Turning to the barman he shouted, "Another round, amigo."

Castro Diaz drew even greater personal satisfaction from the theft of the silver. The Ocotillo Mine was on property that was part of a Spanish land grant awarded to his great grandfather, that was lost in the Gadsden Purchase of 1853. The original property of over 800,000 acres was now a part of the United States and his total wealth had disappeared in the process. He may never get his land back, but at least he would get a few of the benefits of that land. To Castro Diaz, that silver mine belonged to him and his brother Alfredo.

Diaz and Dillon had been stealing ore for several weeks without being detected, or so they thought. Without any guards at the mine at night, they and the peasant "mules" would lug about fifty pounds per man, per night, around the Cody Mt. trail to a central point. There, they would transfer the ore to wagons and move it to San Sebastian, Mexico; then to the smelter. Once the ore reached the smelter, the ore lost its identity and any evidence of theft was destroyed. Cooperative Mexican police were bribed to ensure continuance of the operation safely.

The bandits were confident that a few more midnight raids would provide them with several years worth of easy living. Life in San Sebastian was good.

THE BANK ASSAULT

Major "Turk" Dresser, former commanding officer of the 21st South Carolina Volunteer Regiment, mustered his troops for the assault on the Ribera Mercantile Bank. He had personally scouted the bank and the town, posing as an itinerant horse trader, developing an attack plan. Of equal importance, he'd also mapped out escape routes for the gang for a rendezvous in Mexico.

The major was disappointed that his "troop" of Southern sympathizers had degenerated into a complaining, unsavory rabble, interested only in lining their pockets. Most surprisingly, the enlisted men had repudiated Dresser's goal of re-establishing the Confederacy. The men, in unison, had told the major that "we're worn thin of saving slavery for the cotton planters. They haven't done a damn thing to help the returning veterans who did battle, sometimes being shot up or killed. We'll do the bank job because we've had success in the past, but from now on, we're doing it for our own money belts and not some Jeff Davis slogan."

It was hard for the major to realize that his crew had turned into a band of gangsters; not patriots, intent on re-opening the war against the Union. Facing reality, he assessed his manpower situation. He knew the three former Confederate soldiers would be with him all the way and he trusted the Mexican. Mateo had covered himself well in previous robberies and was steady under pressure. Gus Tomber had quieted down some, but still spent far too much time shadowing LaGrange. Tomber would follow orders until the pie was split up; then he'd cut dirt on his own. Bart LaGrange was still a question mark, but had worked hard to regain his shooting skills. After a week's practice, he could handle his Colt

.44 pistol reasonably well. In a fight, Dresser believed the ex-convict would stand and resist; the prospect of returning to a Texas chain gang was too painful to even think about surrender. "Yes, LaGrange will be a big help on this job; when it's completed, we'll see what happens."

The gang cleared camp and rode into town, splitting into three groups. The soldiers were posted strategically close to the bank, while Mateo moved quickly to engage sheriff Bellows. Sam was half asleep sipping coffee when the Mexican leveled a sawed-off shotgun at his chest and disarmed the lawman. As Mateo tied the sheriff's hands tightly he heard, "Mex, you're making a big mistake. I don't know what you're up to, but you can bet we'll be after you, no matter which way you go." Though he spoke and understood English well, Mateo only grunted "no comprende" and shoved Sam into a jail cell. Before leaving, he knocked the sheriff unconscious with the butt of the shotgun. He then went to the front door, opened it, and signaled to Turk that their phase one plan was successful.

As Brad Scoville was closing up the bank, he was accosted by Turk and Bart LaGrange, while Tomber nonchalantly walked around the side of the bank, holding their getaway horses. It was unusually quiet, due mainly to the heat of the day, and most people being indoors. Turk and Bart pushed Scoville into the bank, closed the door and pulled down the black window shade. Scoville was caught off guard and in a panic when he thought about the amount of paper money, gold and silver coinage that was in the safe. He also realized that the bandits were still undiscovered, armed and dangerous.

Stabbing a pistol barrel into the banker's ribs, Major Dresser ordered Brad to open the safe in the rear room of the bank. Stalling, Scoville complained that the safe had a twelve-hour timer delay in it, and couldn't be opened before early morning, even if he wanted to. "Mr. banker, we're not in any foolin' mood, and you'd best get that box open, and I mean real fast." Dresser's demand was accompanied by a brutal gun barrel blow to the knee, which doubled up the banker. As he collapsed to the carpeted floor, he realized he was in a fight for his life. Writhing in pain, he whispered the combination to Bart, who opened the safe door on the first pass. Pulling the door wide open, both men were shocked to see the cache of coins, cash and gold dust. They worked rapidly to fill gunny sacks and saddle bags with the loot.

Less than five minutes into the robbery, Mateo helped the major and Bart remove the stolen goods to the alleyway, where Gus Tomber held the horses. Shortly joined by the soldiers, the gang saddled up and rode out as a bell began to ring from the steeple on the bank. Crazy over the loss of over $50,000, Scoville had collected his wits, crawled to the bell cord and sounded the alarm that a robbery was taking place.

South of town, on the river where he was on patrol, Buzz Chatham also heard the alarm. Looking northeast to town, he could see a group of horsemen crossing the river apparently en route to the Cimarron Cliffs Trail and the border. Quickly realizing a bank robbery was in progress, the deputy positioned himself near a clump of trees and protective boulders aside the trail and waited. In a matter of minutes, the gang came crashing down the trail, to be met with a rifle shot in the air and a loud "hold it" from Buzz Chatham. Without hesitation, the Dresser gang opened fire to the spot where they saw smoke. Again, random pistol shooting was no match for the deputy's accurate rifle fire. Rapidly squeezing the trigger three times as the riders went flying by, Buzz dropped two of the bandits from their saddles and wounded a third, who managed to stay on his horse with part of the loot as the gang rode south.

Chatham wisely decided he needed help to pursue the robbers, and wanted to examine the two wounded men, now horseless. One man, in a filthy Confederate jacket, was dead from a gun shot to the neck. The other, Gus Tomber, was propped up against a rock wall, immobilized with a serious chest wound. Realizing he was badly hurt, he surrendered to Deputy Chatham, who asked two miners to get a wagon and take the prisoner to Doc Gilroy. "Boys, let's get this hombre to the Doc real fast, this guy's badly hurt."

Nursing a splitting headache, Sheriff Bellows lauded deputy Chatham's brave, prompt action in responding to the bank's alarm. "That damn robbery was slick as a whistle. They were in and out of the bank before anyone in town knew what had happened. It seems like they're on their way to Hachita, so we'd better round up a posse and get movin' at dawn. It looks like Brad Scoville has a busted leg, just below the knee cap, which will keep him on crutches for a while. He's out of his mind worrying about the stolen gold and other stuff and is raising hell over the lack of protection from this office. Only way to quiet him down is to get his money back. We're likely dealing with the Dresser gang, who've been quiet for the past few months. They're in for a big surprise if they think they're safe, just because they made it over the border into Mexico."

Buzz Chatham felt he was part of a law establishment that wasn't doing what they were supposed to do—protect the resources and the citizenry of the community. They'd been too passive in dealing with the miners and let the Newports run things for far too long. Sam was a peace officer who avoided confrontation, and sometimes that didn't work. The bank robbery could be the final straw. "I sure hope we can find whatever his name is in the morning; the town folk are going to be real upset when they hear about this."

The Dresser gang, now five in number, reached the border and the town of Hachita, Sonora, early in the evening. The soldier who was wounded in the escape was being tended to and the gang members were crowing over the success of the robbery. They couldn't believe their good luck and the amount of money to be divided. Losing Tomber and a soldier only added to their anticipation of the split. The loot turned out to be an unexpected bonanza of $60,000. As previously agreed to, the major took 40% of the stickup, which amounted to $24,000. The rest of the money and gold came to $36,000, split equally between Bart LaGrange, Mateo and two others. Not a bad return for an afternoon's work, when a cowhand was making $35 per month, plus room and board.

Bart LaGrange joined the gang for one shot of tequila, happy but scared with his $9,000 robbery money split. He knew the lawmen in Ribera would be getting a posse together and believed that the border with Mexico wouldn't stop them in getting back the bank's money. While the major and gang were hoisting tequila and rounding up a few senoritas, Bart decided to get out of Hachita as soon as possible. The prospect of capture and an extended stay in a Texas state prison only goaded him to leave immediately.

As he retreated from the gang, he was followed by Mateo to the makeshift corral. "Do not draw, Senor Bart, I'm not going to shoot you. I think you are smart to leave the gang now and not wait for morning. The gringo sheriff knows we are here and will come over the border for us in force, whether the Mexican police are here or not. I think a quiet fishing village on the Gulf of California for a year would give us the time to safely lie low. We can talk about that when we are far enough away from here. It is a very long way from here through a terrible desert of 200 miles. Many people have died believing they would find water to survive. I was born and raised in this country. Two people will do better than one man alone. Can we be partners?" Bart looked at the Mexican, nodded in agreement, and the two saddled up and left Hachita to the singing and dancing of the remaining members of the Dresser gang. At the edge of town they filled extra water bags for the dangerous crossing of a desert where daytime temperatures could easily reach 115 degrees.

THE LIEUTENANT

Second Lieutenant Jeremy B. Caswell ordered the troop dismissed, turned and walked to the trading post. The drill had not gone well. Kicking the dust from his boots, he thought about his initial duty assignment to Fort Gore, New Mexico Territory. With the exception of the Indian ambush, his tour had been darn boring. He knew there would be slack periods on the frontier, but in recent weeks, all patrols had been uneventful. Apaches were out there, but rarely seen, and then only at great distances. Food shortages were beginning to take their toll on troop morale; several fights had broken out in the enlisted men's mess. Caswell still savored the beating they had given Aguijador and his warriors, where the chieftain had lost a herd of stolen horses and suffered major casualties. Judging by the more popular stories that permeated the fort, the Apaches should have mounted an attack several weeks ago. Nothing resembling an attack had occurred.

Stepping up to the trading post doorway, he was hailed by Caleb Benson, who ran the store. Jeremy returned the greeting with, "Caleb, I thought this was good country for killing Indians; where in hell have they all disappeared to? Do you think that maybe they've holed up for the winter?"

"Lieutenant, I was just wondering the same thing. I also may have an idea. Old Limping Bear has been around begging me for whiskey; it just might be a good time to find out how much he knows about Aguijador and where he might be hiding."

With Caswell's approval, Caleb put the senior Indian scout on clean-up duty at the trading post, carefully doling out enough whiskey to keep the Indian in a low level stupor. Periodically, he quizzed the old scout every way he knew how, but was unable to squeeze any important information out of him. Exasperated, Caleb decided that Limping Bear was either too smart to reveal any information, or really didn't know. Angry and frustrated, the trader decided it was time to get rid of the Apache, permanently.

Near evening, Caleb bribed two troopers who owed him a lot of money to take Limping Bear for a ride out to the foothills. "Give him a few drinks along the way, be sure he's pretty well skunked and leave him by that large clump of pinon pines. Just leave the whiskey jug with him, that'll give him enough protection from the cold, ha-ha. Whoever finds him in the morning will assume he was off on a drunken spree and froze to death." The troopers, wary that Apaches could be in the area, nervously dropped the Indian off as instructed and quickly turned back to the fort.

As the soldiers galloped away, a pair of Apache Indians, on patrol, witnessed the planned murder and rescued the drunk Army scout from sure death by freezing.

Sergeant Vince Booker was alarmed when he learned that Limping Bear was missing from the fort. Something was seriously wrong. He had worked with the scout on several campaigns and regarded him as an expert tracker, loyal to the U.S. Army. He didn't like the answer he received from Caleb Benson when he asked about the missing scout, nor did he appreciate Lieutenant Caswell's comments. "Sergeant, stop worrying about Limping Bear; he's probably found some firewater and is off someplace getting drunk. He'll be back when he sobers up and gets hungry. Besides, that's one less Apache we have to worry about."

Booker, a seasoned veteran with over twenty years of service, fumed over the lieutenant's remarks and his prejudices to Indians in general. The junior officer was underestimating Apache battle strategy and guerilla tactics. Caswell's first meeting with the Indians had been a well staged ambush because of superior field intelligence, supplied by none other than Limping Bear. It would be a long time before they'd trap any more of Aguijador's warriors.

What worried the sergeant most was Caswell's outspoken belief that the Apaches were cowards to be easily defeated in battle. This mind-set could lead to a military disaster. Wounded twice in Indian battles, Sergeant Booker deeply respected the Apache's bravery, horsemanship and leadership under fire. Besides, he appreciated that the Chiricahua Apaches knew every hill, mountain pass and water hole in the Dragoon Mountains. Somehow, Sergeant Booker knew he had to counter the officer's remarks about Indians being inferior fighters who would turn and run in battle. Some of the older men knew better, but over half of the Fort Gore troopers were still recruits, untested in any campaign. The base commander, Captain Hiram Coolidge, was also inexperienced, and counted on Caswell for battle leadership. Young officers, anxious to be heroes, could lead to dreadful results.

The Apache scouts took Limping Bear, drunk and freezing, to their camp, where Aguijador asked him a series of questions about the fort, status of supplies and ammunition, and how many soldiers were in the garrison. After rest and a hot meal of antelope meat, Limping Bear revealed that the fort was undermanned and short of food and ammunition, awaiting a supply train due in a week or so. The interrogation continued until Aguijador was convinced that Limping Bear had given him all the information he could, including the name of the red-headed officer who had led the ambush. Patrols were set up to maintain surveillance of the main trail to the fort and other Apache tribes alerted to the expectation of the wagon train and convoy on its way to Fort Gore. Apache patience was about to pay off; the food, weapons, ammunition and blankets would serve the tribe well in the coming winter.

While Limping Bear had provided much helpful information, he was also a traitor to the tribal nation. He knew all too well that Apache law demanded the death penalty for treason, but hoped that because of his age and information provided, he would be spared. Limping Bear was mistaken in that assumption.

He was turned over to a trio of ruthless, aspiring warriors who were anxious to mete out tribal justice. They offered the old scout a slim opportunity for freedom. "Sleep well, old man, at dawn you will run for your life. If you can out-run us, you will be free; if we capture you, you will die like a white man: slowly and painfully."

At sunrise, as promised, Limping Bear was given a ten-minute head start, then pursued and hunted down like a wounded animal. It was not a race, let alone fair competition. The young braves tracked and caught Limping Bear when he was near collapse from exhaustion. Without mercy, they stabbed the old man repeatedly with their lances and, closing in, slashed his arms and torso with their razor sharp hunting knives. As the scout lay bleeding to death, one of the enforcers split his skull apart with a battle axe. The bloodied, mutilated body was then lashed to a stolen Army horse and left on the trail leading to the fort. When sentries saw the horse, they opened the gate to find the barely recognizable corpse of Limping Bear. The sight of the mutilated body sent shudders through the fort's defenders, especially the two remaining Apache army scouts.

The sight of the butchered corpse also frightened Caleb Benson; he didn't expect to see Limping Bear die this way. It reminded the trader of stories of Indian brutality and their capacity for revenge. He knew the Apaches would be unmerciful were the fort to fall into their hands. He also pondered how much information Limping Bear gave to Aguijador before he was murdered. He was genuinely scared, but decided not to discuss his fears with the lieutenant. In no way was he about to admit his complicity in the killing of Limping Bear. Furthermore, he would stay clear of Sergeant Booker, who was asking pointed questions about the scout's disappearance and subsequent death.

* * * *

The supply train from Santa Fe had been on the trail for over five weeks, plodding along at ten to twelve miles per day, as long as they didn't have to cross rivers. They'd had several wagon breakdowns, but, protected by a platoon of cavalry, had not encountered any marauding Indians.

After getting through Doubtful Pass without incident, the trail boss relaxed his flank scouting, which was duly noted by a reinforced band of Chiricahua Apache Indians. Over two hundred strong, they waited, composed, for the strike signal from Aguijador. The warriors were well hidden on both sides of the trail, on high ground. As the sun was setting after a toilsome day on the pathway, the Indians launched a rain of arrows and gunfire that startled the surprised convoy troops. They had believed that once past Doubtful Pass, they would be safe.

An overwhelming charge by the Apaches stampeded horses and broke the line of supply wagons into smaller groupings. These individual clusters were attacked fiercely by riders with lances and battle axes. The surprise was complete; the wagon train was captured and most of the guarding soldiers killed or severely wounded. The attackers tore open the wagons to find rifles, ammunition, blankets and food, which was loaded onto pack animals for return to their mountain hideout. Aguijador, the assault leader, praised the work of the attackers. "You warriors have fought bravely and successfully. We have destroyed a rescue supply train headed for Fort Gore, and killed many white faces. We have also captured supplies that will help our women and children survive this winter. This will be the beginning of many more victories for the Apache over the lying white men."

Two survivors of the Apache massacre did make their escape to reach Fort Gore with the devastating news. When they told their story of the attack by the Indians, Lieutenant Caswell was furious; ready to ride out and do battle with the victors. Only darkness and a brief discussion between Sergeant Booker and the commanding officer prevented the foolish attempt to engage a superior force.

Captain Hiram Coolidge, Fort Gore's commanding officer, knew he was in serious trouble. His normal force was reduced to about seventy-five able-bodied troopers, plus a dozen or so civilians, three of whom were women. At best, he had three weeks of reduced rations on hand and was severely short of rifle ammunition. Fort Bliss, Texas, was over two hundred miles east, through mountains infested with Apaches. To the south, there were stray cattle that could be captured and butchered, but Mexican bandits controlled most of the villages. Fort Wingate to the north wasn't even considered. Contact with the presidio at Tucson, eighty miles to the west, through rugged hills and desert, offered the fort its only hope for provisions. Captain Coolidge considered a massive retreat, but decided it would mean the end of the Overland Stage Line and expose Copper flats and Ribera to rampaging Indians. Abandonment of the fort would also signal the end of his army career and a discharge in disgrace.

Coolidge chose to send a few soldiers on a rescue mission to Tucson. The walled town had a population of about seven hundred, eighty percent of whom were Mexican. Only recently acquired by the United States, the people were law abiding, but sympathetic to their old country of Mexico. They also knew that Mexico City, over 1,400 miles to the south, never spent much money to defend the northern extremity of the country. Besides, if Apaches were to overrun Fort Gore, all of southern Arizona would be threatened.

Captain Coolidge would remain at Fort Gore and Lieutenant Caswell would lead four men and an Indian scout to Tucson. They were authorized to purchase needed supplies and arrange for wagons and horses to get the items to the beleaguered fort. If all were to go as planned, the round trip might be completed in a week and a half. Caswell, still smarting from being turned down to chase Aguijador, agreed with the assignment, but fended off a suggestion to have Sergeant Booker accompany him on the mission. Instead, he selected Corporal Shannock and three privates for the dash to Tucson. Captain Coolidge was disappointed in the Lieutenant's choice, but said nothing that would only embarrass the young officer.

Corporal Shannock was a combat trained soldier, but had not been in an actual fire fight with Indians. Privates O'Grady, Preston and Wilson were excellent horsemen, but had little experience on the frontier. An Indian scout, nicknamed Sancho, would be their guide on the relief effort.

Leaving Fort Gore at daybreak, Caswell's party was observed by an Apache sentinel, who promptly relayed the information to Aguijador. The chieftain had anticipated such a move and knew that Tucson would be the shortest, most logical means of getting help. Signaling ahead for added support, he selected a dry wash rendezvous where they would meet and attack the rescue party. Pushing their ponies hard, they were able to reach the position a half hour before the Union troopers arrived.

In the meantime, Lieutenant Caswell's formation rode single file, led by Sancho, into the ambush point. Believing they had slipped away from the fort undetected, the officer called a halt to rest and water their horses, believing they could continue on safely in a couple of hours. A guard was posted, the horses hobbled near good grazing ground and the troop prepared a meal of coffee and biscuits. Sancho, sensing that things were all too quiet, ignored the food offering and stayed close to his horse.

In a lightning strike from two sides, Aguijador and his warriors slammed into the campfire, surprising the soldiers. Rifle fire and lances killed Private O'Grady and wounded the lieutenant, who went down in the soft sand of the river bed. He saw Aguijador bearing down on him, but was unable to pull his pistol out fast enough to avoid a vicious, slashing blow to the neck. As he writhed in pain, the Indian chieftain screamed "vengaza" and plunged his knife into Caswell's chest, killing him. He then proceeded to carefully remove the lieutenant's head of red hair from his body. Only then did he call off the attack.

Corporal Shannock, who was farthest from the campsite when they were attacked, managed to escape the onslaught. Joined by Sancho, they fled the scene as darkness fell. Two days later, the hungry, disheveled pair walked their broken-down horses into Tucson. There they met with Alcalde José Vincenzo, who listened intently to their shocking story. The loss of the wagon train was a serious setback; Vincenzo knew that the food shortages could have a dangerous outcome for Fort Gore and his village. He took the need for food and supplies soberly.

Fearful of an eventual attack on the presidio, the mayor had his two assistants arrange for accumulating food and wagons to help Captain Coolidge and Fort Gore. He also enlisted the support of a dozen local "pistoleros" to escort the wagons to the Army post.

Two weeks after the start of the expedition, the wagon train rolled into Fort Gore, to the resounding cheers of the beleaguered soldiers and civilians. After sorting out the supplies, Captain Coolidge distributed rifle ammunition to his troopers. The captain realized that while they were still short of firepower, they had enough food to last them through the winter months. The captain was pleased to feel that the fort was now capable of survival and had the confidence to ward off Aguijador and his followers.

The loss of Lieutenant Caswell and two troopers greatly disturbed the commander. He reprimanded himself for not insisting that Sergeant Booker go on the rescue mission with the young officer. Youthful exuberance and aggressive decision making were no substitute for good judgment and the need to protect young recruits. More and more, he recognized the importance of field experience. When he promoted Sergeant Booker to Second Lieutenant, he made it clearly known that the newly appointed officer was his second in command. He also instructed Lieutenant Booker to get the Fort Gore troop fully prepared for any Apache spring uprising. The army troop rank and file knew that the hard-driving Booker would be up to the task.

A LETTER HOME

June 6, 1866

Dear Dad:

It seems ages ago that I sat down and wrote you a letter. Saying that I'm too busy really isn't much of an excuse. It was good to hear from Ebbie and know that all is well in Denver.

You now know that Tom's discovery is called the Ocotillo Mine, because the hill is covered with 'em. They are prickly sticks standing five to six feet tall with red tassels at the top. In the springtime, the tassels make a startling sight, like a bright scarlet lure on the end of a fishing rod line. Tom owns 50% and Karl Bruner and me have 25% apiece. Karl is the German engineer I've spoken about earlier who has a lot of experience from working in England and Mexico. He has already expanded our number of claims and mapped the geology of the area around the mine. At the rate we are going, I think we will be able to return your $5,000 loan, with some interest, in a month or so. I agree with your decision to leave the mining to us; it's very time consuming and risky. While I believe we have a profitable operation in the making, many things could happen to upset our plans. There's no sense jeopardizing your retirement money either.

I'm spending most of my time at the mine, getting several buildings put up that will enable us to house and feed at least a half dozen miners, a cook and sleeping quarters for Tom, Konrad and me. It's definitely not the Brown Palace, but sure beats sleeping out in the open, listening to javelinas scrounging for food. The foraging coati-mundis can also make a racket. They travel in packs and look something like a raccoon with a long curled-up tail.

The ore that has been removed from the tunnel is all high grade. Where it's heavy in native silver, we easily run about $800 to the ton. We have over three hundred tons on the ground, waiting for delivery to the smelter in Copper City, which is about twenty-five miles from here. Once we start regular deliveries, we should begin to turn a profit and stop depleting the money that Konrad has put in. That's when we will be able to pay you off. Our most pressing problem has been getting a bridge built over Growler Creek, but I think Barney Pryor, a local teamster, has got that obstacle solved. Barney is one of those guys that you meet once in a while who quietly seems to get things done without a lot of fanfare. We could use a few more people like him.

On the bad news side, we've found out that poachers have been stealing from our stockpile. We think it's a group of Mexicans who take the ore over the border to a gypsy smelter. We've talked to the Ribera sheriff, but he won't help us. "Look, I sympathize with you guys, but problems between the Newports and the miners are a much higher priority for me. I can't be in two places at once, especially when they're twenty miles apart. Try the sheriff at Copper Flats; if that doesn't work, you'll have to deal with things by yourselves."

So we've hired a couple of ex-Union soldiers to handle guard duty for us. A new main building will house expensive supplies and will have a reinforced cage to store some of the ore. The poachers are probably coming up from Old Mexico, back-packing our stuff out to a central point, then using a wagon and teamsters to take over and get the loot over the border. At fifty pounds per man each night, ten hungry Mexicans could steal us blind in no time.

The Ocotillo Mine has kept me on the run and away from practicing medicine. I helped Doc Gilroy (you'd like this guy, Dad) patch up a few of the wounded in a recent shoot-out between the miners and the River Bank Ranch people, but that's about all. When I'm not at the mine, I'm on the lookout for experienced hard rock miners, or getting the road to Copper City in shape. Most of the placer miners near Tent City prefer panning for gold to make the strike that will make them rich. Hard rock mining is far rougher work and unfortunately, sometimes dangerous, so it's not easy to get men to join us at Growler Creek. The presence of some civilization in Ribera doesn't help our cause any either. As long as the river continues to produce gold, we will have trouble getting the people we need. Doc Gilroy has asked me to join up with him, but I've committed a year to Tom and the mine, so doctoring will have to wait a while, I guess.

I'd like to tell you that Tom and I have become close again, but I'd be stretching the truth. We eat together only once in a while, and when we do, we talk about personnel shortages, problems in the mine and the theft of the ore, of course. Tom works the mine ten to twelve hours a day and expects everyone to have the same commitment. He'll go into town for tools and equipment, but rarely stays long enough for a meal at the hotel. The mine is his life. He still has misgivings about partnering with Konrad and hasn't fully accepted the German, in spite of all the good things he's done for the operation. At times, I'm not sure he wants me as a partner either. He's a loner, bent on becoming a mining baron, is the best way to explain it, I guess. But I also admire his drive to get the mine up and running; it's hard, dirty work.

The mine at times is full of surprises. Recently, we ran into a problem; we'd been following the vein, cutting the tunnel as we went along. Then we ran into a fault zone, which is an area developed when two rock masses rub against each other, creating a conglomeration of broken debris. The zone turned out to be barren, which really scared us. What happened to the vein? By examining the country rock and studying the various layers of limestone and sandstone, Konrad was able to figure out that block faulting had caused an offset of eight to ten feet. In other words, the vein was cut and displaced that amount below our existing tunnel. To prove his theory, Karl drilled an exploratory hole at an angle, and rediscovered the main vein. Tom was happy to be back in business, but still doesn't believe that what happened wasn't just plain dumb luck. This may sound like mumbo jumbo to you, but I believe Konrad knows mining and will continue to be a big asset to the company; he knows what he is doing. Tom remains skeptical of the German's university training, but I'm avoiding taking any sides in the discussions, which sometimes get heated. The important thing is we are back in full operation.

The town of Ribera continues to grow. Being on the only stage line between El Paso and Tucson has attracted discharged army people from both sides, homesteaders and a raft of derelicts who only add to the general disorder and turbulence in the community. Add in the California miners who have worked the Yuma area and moved here on news that there's placer gold in the Bowie River. It's been a stampede. I'd guess we have two to three hundred of them in a place we call Tent City, digging and sifting sand and gravel, hoping to find gold. A few have been successful, but most, after a few weeks, get discouraged, and move on to the next "hot spot" rumor. That happens to be the Prescott area, which is about two hundred miles northwest of here. Many of these men are former military, still arguing and fighting over the results of the Civil War. The gold also attracts desperados intent on stealing whatever has been taken from the river.

A week or so ago, we had a bank robbery, which still has people talking. Led by a retired rebel army officer, the gang hit our Mercantile Bank, making off with about $60,000 in gold dust, silver coin, paper currency and bank notes taken from the safe. The bank president was severely beaten in the fracas when he refused to reveal the combination to the safe. Eventually of course, he did. Fortunately, the Deputy Sheriff heard the alarm go off and intercepted the gang, killing one and wounding two others. Most of the town folk thought Buzz Chatham was a weak sister, but now look at him as a real hero. One wounded robber confessed to the rendezvous point, and the following morning, a large posse led by the sheriff and Buzz crossed into Old Mexico and captured the leader and most of the gang members. Two riders in the posse received minor wounds; about $40,000 of the stolen money was recovered. The Mexicans in Hachita were unhappy over U.S. nationals crossing the border, but couldn't offer any resistance. For once, Sheriff Bellows took firm action and saved most of the bank's money.

I helped Doc Gilroy work on Brad Scoville's leg, which was broken below the knee. His kneecap was also smashed in the assault, so we had our work cut out for us. I think we did a good job, but am afraid that Brad will be limping for the rest of his life. On balance though, he's lucky to be alive; Major Dresser's gang were a mean bunch.

I should also tell you that I've met a wonderful young lady from Tennessee, who works and lives with her aunt, who owns the local general store. She's twenty years old, medium height, brown hair, and very attractive. Her passion is raising horses and of course, she is an excellent rider and roper. Her name is Kate Hurley and while raised in the South, she is vehemently opposed to slavery. I know that you and Ebbie would like her as much as I do.

I hope this letter finds you and Ebbie in good health. We look forward to hearing from you and the possibility of a visit from you.

Your loving son,
Ben

THE POACHERS

Hostilities between the ranchers and the miners had thankfully receded to a cease-fire. However, it was a fragile truce. Ranch hands and diggers avoided one another in town; the miners respected stakes on the riverbank, outlining River Bend Ranch property. Ribera townsfolk began to breathe a sigh of relief and go about their normal business. Thanks to the establishment of a non-partisan Bowie River Water Board, both parties were receiving adequate water for their activities. The idea of a water board had come from Don Richmond, son-in-law of Dale Newport, who had emerged as a respected leader to town officials during negotiations.

The dam was to remain in place, with fifty percent of the river water diverted to the miners in daylight hours; at sundown, the full flow of the river would be allocated for the benefit of the River Bend Ranch.

The miners returned to their claims and quickly resumed sorting sand, grit and gravel, searching for the valuable specks of gold. Konrad Bruner and Peter Hillenbrand were most pleased of all the interested parties. Plotting a grid over the newly acquired land east of the existing workings, Bruner had methodically sampled the property owned by the partners. Exploratory pits had been dug to a depth of four feet; the sand and gravel quartered and bagged. The bagged material was then taken to an off-site shed for examination. Most of the miners had no idea what the German engineer was up to, nor did they care; they were too busy with their own prospecting.

The results of Konrad's efforts were encouraging. As he remarked to "PH," "I think we have enough metal showing from our samples to make us both rich.

Our job now is to keep our findings secret until we can organize an operation to process the ground we have."

Dale Newport was subdued and had little to say when Sheriff Sam Bellows visited him at the ranch. He was still grieving over the loss of his son and embarrassed over his own loss of power and influence in the community. His inability to "even the score" with the miners only added to his discomfort. The fact that he had encouraged Greg to start the fight distracted him to the point of being unable to do much of anything.

His brooding cast a pall over the ranch. He stopped riding the fence lines and avoided all day-to-day work responsibilities. Garland Newport and her daughter gradually filled the void of running the household; Don Richmond took over the job of wrangler foreman with considerable success. In short order, the men respected his competence and learned to even like working for the man. Stray cattle were rounded up and branded, fences mended and corrals and buildings repaired. Not being needed, and sometimes ignored, Dale Newport retreated to his office and sipped whiskey most of the day.

Sam Bellows knew that many of the town people were unhappy over recent developments and his performance. The river fight had taken several lives and a few of the walking wounded would never return to full-time ranch work. And, the miners were still free from prosecution. Lacking solid eyewitness testimony as to who fired the fatal shots that killed Greg Newport, the sheriff had chosen to close the case, without jailing a single person.

At the request of the Water Board, Buzz Chatham patrolled the damsite while water was being diverted to the miners. It seemed to be working; no serious incidents had occurred.

Things were coming to a boil, though, at Growler Creek. Stopping by the Whitman Hotel saloon after a day at the damsite, Deputy Buzz Chatham had overheard boastful comments made by Val Higgins, the town boozer. Fueled by a few free drinks from a winning gambler, Val had laughed as to how the Lawson brothers were doing at the Ocotillo Mine. "Hell, those dudes are mining ore for someone else to steal. Why, them tenderfoots don't know the first thing about mining, let alone protecting themselves from poachers. Those Mexi's have been raiding that pile of ore for over two weeks without gettin' caught. By golly, those boys must be blind." The more he listened, the more Buzz Chatham became convinced that maybe Val knew what he was talking about. At the very least, it demanded an investigation. This wasn't the time or place to question Val Higgins, but he'd sure discuss what he'd heard with the sheriff.

A conversation with the sheriff led Sam Bellows to leave Ribera and visit the Lawson brothers and the Ocotillo Mine. The river was quiet and he knew Buzz could be trusted to act responsibly, if problems came up. As he rode into the mine yard, he heard, "Well, well, what brings you up this way, Sam? I thought we were off limits to you lawmen."

"Tom, you surely knew we were in no position to leave town with all the problems on the river. I think you'll be interested in what we've discovered regarding your shrinking ore pile. Things are a little quieter in town and I thought I could lend a hand to you men."

After Bellows described what Buzz and he had learned, Tom became very interested in the sheriff's remarks. The Ocotillo Mine, at 5,800 feet, lay on the flanks of Mt. Cody, which towered to 9,200 feet in elevation. The peak of the mountain was usually snow covered, nine months of the year. Huge white pine and ponderosa pine trees provided a green canopy over a narrow trail that stretched from Growler Creek to a flatland called Pradera Verde, or green meadow. From this level spot, the trail widened and meandered through manzanita and scrub oak trees, to San Sebastian, Old Mexico. In early years, the trail was heavily used by miners, working small properties. The trail had seen little use in recent years.

Tom Lawson showed the sheriff how the ore was handled and stored, waiting for Barney Pryor's wagons to move it to Copper Flats and the smelter. With a minimum of searching, they found the trail marks and followed the beaten track south to Pradera Verde. The area appeared to be deserted. It didn't take Tom and the sheriff long to locate the cache of silver ore in a shallow grave, near a cluster of prickly pear and mesquite bushes. Examining a couple of chunks of ore, Tom spotted green paint on several pieces, confirming that indeed it was stolen goods from the Ocotillo Mine. When Tom explained to Sam how his brother had coated fragments of ore with green paint, the sheriff agreed that they had sufficient evidence to confiscate the treasure and arrest the thieves.

Leaving Sam Bellows at the collection point, Tom rode back to the mine to enlist the help of two ex-soldiers, who would form part of the welcoming committee for the Mexican poachers. Tom and the sheriff agreed that a full moon, clear night operation for the poachers would be an ideal situation for the miners to capture the thieves.

Their guess on weather conditions proved to be an accurate one. As dusk approached, the sheriff placed Tom and his two miners in a semi-circle surrounding the hidden hoard, while Sam stationed himself where the trail entered the meadow. The plan called for Bellows to signal Tom and his men when the poachers started to load up their wagon, to take it to San Sebastian.

It wasn't long before the sheriff, and then Tom, heard the creaking wheels of a heavy wagon, making its way up the trail. The crooks were certain their work would be completed without mishap and were bantering back and forth in Spanish. Sam allowed the troop to pass by him before alerting Tom with the call of an owl. Four hoots indicated that four men were in the group, accompanying the wagon. As the gang began to load the carrier, Sam Bellows shouted, "Tire el armas!" (Drop the guns!) at the poachers. Astonished, the thieves attempted to scatter, yelling "no dispare" (don't shoot), as they drew pistols and fired wildly towards the sheriff's voice. In response, Tom and the well-hidden miners opened fire on the filchers, wounding one and chasing the others back to where Sam Bellows was hidden near the trail entrance. Kneeling, the sheriff fired his Winchester at the apparent leader, who was doing most of the shouting and directing. His two shots felled the man, while two of his companions raced frantically down the trail and their escape. Tying the severely wounded thief to the wagon, the sheriff called out to Tom and the miners to "cease fire." They decided to wait until the following sun-up to seek medical aid for the gang leader. This decision probably cost Castro Diaz his life.

The following morning, Tom returned to the site of the gunfight to start packing the regained silver ore for return to their stockpile. Using leather sacks, they loaded up two mules and the miners left the meadow. "Sam, I'm much obliged for all your help last night. We were pretty lucky; we got the leader, who is now dead, and his friend is up at the mine, licking his wounds. He'll make it, thanks to Brother Ben's medicine." Sam nodded, "The body of the leader has a moustache and a thick scar on his left hand, which tells me he's Castro Diaz, member of a prominent family in Old Mexico. His brother runs the family empire from a ranch about a hundred and fifty miles down the trail from Tubac. Even though Castro has been a wanted man for over a year, for cattle rustling and a killing, his death won't sit well with his brother."

As Tom was finishing the return of the silver ore, Sam suggested that he bury Castro in the meadow where the ore was collected. If the family wanted to exhume the corpse, and return it to Mexico, they'd know where to direct them. "The more I think about the Castro death, the more I'm concerned that the brother will be looking for all of us. They don't take a family death lightly, even if it's well deserved."

Down in San Sebastian, the two survivors of the gun battle went over the disaster again; while Franco Lopez, owner of the cantina, and Alfred Diaz listened intently. As they sat at a heavy wood circular table, drinking tequila, Alfredo's blood pressure began to rise. "You scum of the earth were paid to steal the ore and protect my brother and you have failed on both counts. And my brother is dead. You two will also pay the price that he has." Slipping his hand to his pistol under the table, Alfredo fired a lethal shot into one of the men, while Lopez clubbed the second from behind with a heavy wooden bat. Alfredo stood up and calmly drilled two shots into the second, unconscious, unfortunate man. "Franco, get rid of this sewage and send someone to Ribera to get my brother's body. I want to know who killed him. I'll be at the ranch awaiting your message."

VENGEANCE

Sam Bellows changed his mind. Digging a decent grave to ward off animal scavengers was hard work and Sam wanted to be certain that the deceased really was Castro Diaz. He would have Doc Gilroy do the examining and prepare the body for burial. Rigor mortis had set in, so he borrowed a buggy from the Lawsons for the trip back to Ribera.

Reading recent criminal circulars, the sheriff was sure that the body he delivered to Doc Gilroy was Castro Diaz. With a medical report signed by Gilroy, Sam sent a message to Santa Fe, requesting the "dead or alive" reward of $500, a sum that would cover medical exams and funerals for the future in town. Until the reward money was received, Doc would have to wait for payment for his services. Most people looked at spending any burial money on crooks and vagrants as a complete waste of time and money.

The Doc wasn't surprised when a representative of the Diaz family showed up at his office. The courier asked questions about Castro's death, but didn't press the issue when Gilroy referred him to the sheriff. After viewing the corpse, Emilio identified the body as that of Castro Diaz and asked to return him to Old Mexico and a Catholic funeral. Doc Gilroy readily acceded to the request, had Emilio sign a receipt and released the cadaver, discharging him from any further responsibility.

Alfredo Diaz was infuriated and over-excited. He'd involved his younger brother in an ill-fated robbery that appeared to be safe and simple and now he was dead. Though unconfirmed, he believed Tom Lawson and Sheriff Sam Bellows killed his brother. He took his brother to Bituminoso, a small village where his parents lived. His mother was heart-broken when he arrived and refused to believe that her son had died a natural death. Father Marcos was also skeptical, but out of consideration for the senior Diaz family, provided a high mass funeral service. After the funeral, Alfredo spent several days with his parents, who blamed the older brother for Castro's early demise, refusing to believe the rumors that their younger son was a fugitive from justice.

Alfredo's plan to use some of the money from the theft of Lawson ore to re-stock his herd was now a shambles. He was still land rich, but had virtually no cash to run the ranch. After mulling over his limited options, he decided to avenge his brother first and worry about the ranch later on. Fretting and periodically fuming, he decided to settle on the destruction of the Ocotillo Mine, preferably with the Lawson brothers in it.

He also liked the idea because in his heart, he believed the mine was on property given to his grandfather in the 1700's by a special grant from the King of Spain. The land grant of over 800,000 acres had been voided by the Gadsden Purchase and Treaty of Hidalgo in 1854. "May Santa Anna rot in his grave for taking a paltry $10 million for over 300,000 hectares of beautiful mountains, farm land and desert in southern Arizona." As he simmered down he decided to plot his course of action carefully; the gringos might anticipate a "venganza con furia" (violent act of vengeance).

He knew little about the Lawson brothers and Konrad Bruner; only that they were newcomers to the territory. Cunningly, he decided to approach gaining access to the mine directly. He was sure that they didn't know him or suspect that he was involved in the theft of the silver ore. Riding into the mine area, he told one of the miners that he was looking for work. He was referred to Konrad Bruner, who was in the mine office working on siting a location for a head frame. Concealing his ability to speak and understand English, Alfredo addressed the German in Spanish.

"Senor Bruner, I have come here from Fresnillo, where I worked as a miner on the Pitada property. I am experienced in the drilling, blasting and mucking of ore. I am a hard worker who will do a good job for you and earn your respect. I am also hungry and tired from the trip and could start right away. I carry all my belongings with me." Konrad was impressed with the man's credentials and decided to hire him on the spot. He did not have the bearing of a peasant or uneducated worker, and seemed to know enough about hard rock mining. Besides, they were desperate for laborers. Tom Lawson's reaction was, "This is too good to be true; let's put him to work."

Over the next few weeks, Alfredo studied the mine operations, timbering in the tunnel, blasting procedures and removal of ore and waste material. He noted that most of the time, Tom Lawson or the German engineer were on-site when the day shift ended and preparations were made for blasting. Usually, one or the other supervised placement of the charges, and configuration of the fuse cord. When the mine was then vacated, the fuse was ignited and the explosion occurred. After the blast, the mine was kept vacant overnight to let the dust settle and allow the fumes to be evacuated. Actually, he was very impressed with the safety procedures employed.

All blasting components and equipment were kept in a bunker that had metal doors, firmly secured under lock and key. The only people who could access the powder magazine were Tom Lawson, Konrad and Stefano, an experienced and trusted hard rock miner. By "helping" Stefano and the mine owners, Alfredo learned the various procedures involved, including spacing of the drill holes, placement of the charges and ignition of the powder. Both Tom and Konrad were pleased to see the interest and diligence exhibited by the new man. Alfredo patiently bided his time, searching for the opportunity to complete his mission.

It was the end of the shift; holes had been bored and the face of the tunnel prepared for blasting. Best of all, both Konrad and Tom were away from the mine, and not expected to return until early evening. During the day's drilling, Alfredo had instructed the miners to deepen the holes, as "suggested" by Tom Lawson. While Tom had not given the orders, they assumed he actually had, and did what they were told to do. Besides, the owners were away, Stefano wasn't around and Alfredo always seemed to know what he was doing.

Six well-spaced holes had been drilled in the face of the ore body. Stefano returned and opened the bunker and removed explosives to fill the holes with the black powder mixture. Stefano was happy to let Alfredo set the charges and walked out of the tunnel while Diaz completed the ignition plan. "My God, it's hot here," lamented Stefano as he walked to the water barrel for a drink.

Alfredo filled each hole with powder and tamped the charge with sand. He then connected all six holes to a single line and slowly walked backwards toward the mouth of the tunnel. Suddenly, he turned to see Tom Lawson near the opening of the tunnel, talking to Stefano, who was waving his arms, pointing at Alfredo. When Tom approached Alfredo, the Mexican only shrugged when asked, "What's going on here? Why are you setting the charges?" When Alfredo replied, "No comprende, senor Tom," Tom began to inspect Alfredo's work with the explosives and detonating cord. As Tom bent over to examine the connections, Alfredo grabbed a heavy shovel and clubbed him into unconsciousness.

Quickly, he grabbed the end of the detonating cord and lit it. As the cord began to sputter, Alfredo dashed for his life, realizing that the short cordage would only allow him a matter of seconds before exploding. He was barely close to the tunnel mouth when he felt the heated blast and concussion.

Alfredo was blown off his feet as the earth rumbled and debris discharged from the mine opening. As a small group of miners stood in shocked bewilderment, Alfredo picked himself up, ran for his horse, jumped astride the animal and galloped south towards Old Mexico. Hopefully, he would have some protection in his mother country.

As the trail became a rocky passage, Alfredo reined in and allowed the gelding to walk carefully. He turned to see a large gray cloud, hovering where the mine was located. He didn't experience the expected elation and excitement he thought he'd get from destroying the Ocotillo Mine and the death of Tom Lawson. "Would Father Marcos allow forgiveness for premeditated murder?"

Karl Bruner was looking over a prize stallion at the Volunteer Ranch when he heard the distant, muffled explosion. From the direction it came and the rising plume of gray and black smoke, he knew the blast had occurred at the Ocotillo Mine. Barbara Casey read the expression on Konrad's face and also figured that there was trouble at the mine, a distant five miles away. "Barbara, that explosion had to come from the mine; I don't know what the problem is, but I'd better get over there as quickly as I can. Someone may be hurt. I was looking forward to a quiet dinner with you, but I'd better get going to see just what the problem is. If Ben happens to come by, tell him I'll meet him at the mine."

"Konrad, don't worry one bit about dinner; it will keep until you get back." As Konrad climbed on his horse, she smiled and said, "Good luck, Konrad, I hope you don't run into serious problems." As he gradually drifted out of sight, she mused, "In some ways, he so reminds me of my Tom. He's a kind, considerate person that gets along well with most people. Is it possible that this might lead to something? Good Lord, am I getting serious about this man?"

As he scrambled up the rise to the mine, Konrad was shocked to see the camp in disarray. The smoke had not cleared from the tunnel and he didn't see Tom anywhere. The men were shouting for Senor Tom, but no one seemed to be doing anything to find out where he was. When one miner kept pointing to the tunnel opening, Konrad felt a knot in his stomach, knowing that Tom was still inside the passageway. Instinctively, Konrad dismounted, covered his mouth with a bandana and ran into the tunnel. Almost immediately, he bumped into a fallen timber that stopped his further entry. The tunnel was filled with dust and acrid fumes that prevented Konrad from seeing anything. His shouts for Tom received no reply. Gasping for air, he dropped to his knees and slowly groped his way down the passageway until he bumped into an eight-inch square timber that blocked further access. Carefully he squeezed under the heavy post.

As he wormed his way forward, Konrad touched the unconscious form of Tom Lawson. Realizing the serious threat of contaminated air, Konrad seized Tom by the shirt collar, reversed course and dragged Tom to the mine entryway and fresh air. Gasping for clean air, he checked Tom's breathing and decided that he was seriously hurt and needed medical attention. He spoke repeatedly to the injured man, but got no response.

Beckoning to Gaspar, he ordered, "Ride down to Ribera as fast as you can. Find Doc Gilroy and tell him that Tom has been hurt bad in a mine explosion and needs your help. If you see Ben along the way, tell him the same story and to get to the Volunteer Ranch as quick as you can. We'll get Tom over there in the meantime; now vamos!"

As Gaspar hurtled down the riverbed to Ribera, Bruner gathered blankets from the main office and told two of the miners to hitch a team of mules to one of the empty ore wagons. Guardedly, they loaded Tom into the bed of the wagon and began their descent to cross the creek and the Bowie River. And hour later, they wheeled into the ranch house compound of the Volunteer Ranch. As they eased the injured man out of the wagon, they were met by an anxious Barbara Casey. "Barbara, he's hurt pretty bad; I sure hope that the doctors show up real soon. He's barely breathing."

"Konrad, let's get him into the living room; we've got a bed ready that will keep him warm. I've got bandages if needed and I'll have plenty of hot water ready for the doctors when they get here. Now sit down and have some coffee, you look exhausted." As he sipped the hot fluid, Konrad explained that things were pretty confused.

"All I know is that Alfredo was in the mine setting a charge when Tom walked in. The next thing, there was an explosion and Alfredo was running out of the mine, jumping on a horse and bee-lining it for San Sebastian. Apparently, Tom was still inside the tunnel when it happened. When I got to the mine, the men were still milling around in a daze. When I asked Tom's whereabouts, they could only point to the mine opening, now filled with smoke and fumes. Stefano was the only one who kept his head and helped me get Tom out of the mine. Something's amiss with Alfredo, running off the way he did, but that questioning will have to wait. It'll be a day or so before the air clears in the mine and we can assess the damage. In the meantime, let's hope that one of doctors gets here before it's too late."

Doc Gilroy was the first to arrive, shortly followed by Ben Lawson. Doc Gilroy stood aside while Ben made a quick but thorough examination of his injured brother. Turning to Gilroy, Ben said, "Doc, there's not much we can do. This had to be a damn big explosion. Tom's lungs are seared, he's got broken ribs and one helluva injury to his head and neck. I've seen a few blast patients in the lead mines of Missouri and when injured like this, they rarely survive. Unfortunately, there's very little we can do; it's probably a blessing that Tom is unconscious. The pain from the internal burns and injuries can be horrible. This will break Dad's heart."

Doc Gilroy checked over Tom again, but reluctantly agreed that they were fighting a losing battle. Tom Lawson died a few minutes later, without ever regaining consciousness. Ben Lawson, with tears in his eyes, shook his head when Doc Gilroy opened a silver flask to take a swig of whiskey. Ben had experienced people dying as a physician, but never expected to witness the accidental death of his brother at this stage of his life. Gloom settled over the ranch as the two doctors prepared Tom's body for removal to Ribera.

Tom's death shocked Ben Lawson deeply. While he was younger than Tom, he somehow felt responsible for his brother's untimely death. He tortured himself by wondering if he had been at the mine when the explosion occurred, he might have been able to save his brother. It didn't occur to him until days later, after Sam Bellows's investigation, that Tom had been murdered by a Mexican national seeking revenge.

The accident and Tom's premature death did convince Ben that he would recommit himself to the field of medicine. Getting rich wasn't all he wanted from life.

EPILOGUE
▼

It is six o'clock in the morning; the sun is igniting the sky over Mt. Cody, twenty miles away, as dawn is breaking. Both physicians are exhausted, after spending most of the night with Maggie Bronson, who has been laboring over twenty hours to give birth to a child. When a daughter arrives with a loud scream, the doctors and parents are thrilled with a live healthy baby. Joe Bronson scans his first newborn, silently counting toes and fingers, thanks the doctors profusely, kisses his semi-conscious wife and stumbles to the door to go home for a rest. "Thanks, gents, and may God bless you both."

The young mother and child are placed in a bed and crib, so that they too will be allowed to capture some well-deserved sleep. The two doctors pour a second cup of coffee, look at one another and sit down for the first time since the Bronsons knocked at the door of the clinic, early the previous evening.

"Ben, I've probably delivered over a hundred children over the past forty years, but this was by far the most difficult and challenging. I confess, I wasn't sure mother and child were going to make it. Without the new equipment and your skill with the forceps, I don't think Mrs. Bronson or the baby would have survived. I'm sure glad we decided to expand my place with a new room to be a hospital room, however modest." With that admission, Doc Gilroy rubs his stubbled chin and yawns loudly.

Dr. Ben Lawson quietly nods his approval. "Doc, don't be so modest; your contribution was critical." Shifting to another subject, Ben adds, "These past three years here in Ribera have been the busiest and most gratifying a man could expect, and a lot of that is due to you sharing your knowledge of medicine, but more important, your common sense. The town certainly is not without its problems, but think about the progress we've been able to make."

*   *   *   *

In point of fact, the town had made remarkable progress in the past three years. The most important event was the agreement to share the water of the Bowie River, reached by a newly formed Water Board, the River Bend Ranch and the miners near Tent City. On a more controlled basis, the miners continued to sift sand and gravel in the river bed, searching for gold. The banks of the river were also more clearly defined and respected by both parties.

While Dale Newport refused to sign the agreement and groused about the presence of the miners until he died, the compromise allowed the town to heal and move on. It also revealed leadership qualities in Don Richmond that would eventually propel him into state politics.

The Ocotillo Mine explosion and death of Tom Lawson were a second event in the young history of Ribera. After the death of Tom, Sam Bellows singlehandedly rode into Old Mexico, boldly arrested Alfredo Diaz and brought him to trial. Alfredo was convicted of premeditated murder and died on the gallows in 1868. Due to recent successes with criminal activity in the area, Sam was elected to office, which turned into lifetime employment for the peace officer. Buzz Chatham became sheriff of Copper Flats, when Mike Timmerman retired.

The Ocotillo Mine tragedy forced Ben Lawson to decide what he really wanted from life. He returned to the practice of medicine and married Kate Hurley, settling down in the town of Ribera by taking over Doc Gilroy's old residence and office. In 1869, Kate and Ben became proud parents of Tom II and Rachel, both now two years old. The elder doctor was happy to partially retire and move into Mrs. Cawley's boarding house.

After the mine disaster, Konrad Bruner became mine manager and over a period of six months, restored the damaged facility to normal. In the next two years, production was resurrected and shipments of ore were made on a regular basis to the smelter in Copper Flats. In time, Barney Pryor became the mine's administrative manager and a minor partner to Konrad and Ben.

Konrad's placer gold prospect, in partnership with Peter Hillenbrand, developed into a major production unit, run by Dan Sullivan and a crew of six miners. Using modern water guns, the discovery began consistently producing over 100 ounces of gold per week. Once the sand and gravel were processed, Bruner insisted that the tailings be returned to their natural architecture, making the operation one of America's first environmental reconstruction projects. It also enabled Konrad Bruner to enter the real estate business with improved building lots for sale, sometimes on the water.

As the Tent City gold deposit prospered, Konrad gained majority ownership in the Ocotillo Mine as Ben became a silent, minority associate. By 1870, Konrad Bruner's name and wealth status were well known throughout the state.

When Peter Hillenbrand announced that he was returning to New York, the community was shocked, but not surprised. The town's consensus was that while "PH" had given the West a try, he never really adapted to the hardships of cattle ranching and mining. The shortage of "decent females" only compounded his desire to leave Ribera. Leaving in haste cost the New Yorker dearly. He accepted a $35,000 buyout in cash from Konrad Bruner that was worth ten times that amount if he would patiently take a percentage of the placer mining over a five-year period. Declining that offer, he took the cash and arranged to get to San Francisco for a vacation and eventual clipper ship passage to the East Coast. Barbara Casey never received the down payment for the sale of her general store, and by default, retained ownership in her emporium.

Brad Scoville's Mercantile Bank did well in the late 1860's and he was able to build a new stone facility using local limestone. With a state-of-the-art vault and new security measures in place, he was confident that there would not be a recurrence of a major bank robbery. The missing money, most likely stolen by Bart LaGrange and his Mexican compadre, was never recovered. It remained a mystery as to how they escaped the sheriff's posse and vanished. Most likely, they attempted to cross the desert to California, but never made it; their bones bleaching where they fell, dying from thirst and heat stroke.

Bart LaGrange and Mateo Jiminez did, in reality, cross the Sonoran Desert and survive. Finding their way to the Sea of Cortez, the duo drifted south along the coast, carefully avoiding Mexican police. Assuming new identities and maintaining low profiles, they gradually blended into the local community of Puerto Spinoza. Here, they bought fertile, well-irrigated farmland, unique to western Mexico, and established themselves as successful growers. They also married, raised families and became life-long business partners and close personal friends.

As Ribera grew and matured, the U.S. Army steadily increased its influence and control of Indian Territories in the Southwest. When the Civil War ended, damaged forts were repaired, new stockades constructed and additional manpower was transferred to the West to defeat the Apaches. The surrender and treatment of the Navajos after their capitulation at Canyon de Chelly convinced Aguijador that their only hope for survival as a nation was to continue fighting; never to give in to the white man's threats and promises. It would take many years and the spilling of much blood before this proud assemblage would be subdued.

ABOUT THE AUTHOR

George E. Smith has been employed in the mining industry for over thirty-five years. As a resident of Arizona, he has worked as an exploration geologist, ran a mining company and consulted with several Indian tribal leaders.

978-0-595-46084-7
0-595-46084-4